Designing Engineering Solutions

Inventors of Transportation Technology

Heather S. Morrison

Cavendish Square
New York

Published in 2016 by Cavendish Square Publishing, LLC
243 5th Avenue, Suite 136, New York, NY 10016

First Edition

Website: cavendishsq.com

CPSIA Compliance Information: Batch #WS15CSQ

Cataloging-in-Publication Data

Morrison, Heather S.
Inventors of transportation technology / by Heather S. Morrison.
p. cm. — (Designing engineering solutions)
Includes index.
ISBN 978-1-50260-662-4 (hardcover) ISBN 978-1-50260-663-1 (ebook)
1. Transportation engineering — Juvenile literature. 2. Inventors — Juvenile literature. 2. I. Morrison, Heather S. II. Title.
TA1149.M73 2016
629.04—d23

The author would like to thank the following contributors: Richard Beatty, Laura Lambert, Paul Schellinger, Mary Sisson, Chris Woodford

Editorial Director: David McNamara
Editor: Kristen Susienka
Copy Editor: Michele Suchomel-Casey
Art Director: Jeffrey Talbot
Designer: Alan Sliwinski
Senior Production Manager: Jennifer Ryder-Talbot
Production Editor: Renni Johnson
Photo Research: J8 Media

The photographs in this book are used by permission and through the courtesy of: ID1974/Shuterstock.com, cover, 1; Tetra Images/Getty Images, 4; Liszt Collection/Heritage Images/Getty Images, 6; ArchMan/Shutterstock.com, 12; Dzika_Mrowka/iStock/Thinkstock, 14; Public domain, 16; Pubdog/File:Trico Plant No. 1 Dec 09.jpg/Wikimedia Commons, 18; DeAgostini/Getty Images, 19; Fronteras/File:Karl Benz Automobile.jpg/Wikimedia Commons, 21; Radu Razvan/Shutterstock.com, 25; Patti McConville/Photographer's Choice/Getty Images, 27; Courtesy Automotive Hall of Fame, 28; Illegitimate Barrister/File:1973 Oldsmobile Toronado Custom, Gaithersburg, Maryland, June 29, 2009.jpg/Wikimedia Commons, 30; Wladyslaw/File:Daimler Reitwagen.jpg/Wikimedia Commons, 33; National Motor Museum/Heritage Images/Getty Images (left), SSPL/Getty Images (right), 34; Taina Sohlman/Shutterstock.com, 36; Reinhard Tiburzy/Shutterstock.com, 39; SSPL/Getty Images, 40; Rainer Plendl/Shutterstock.com, 45; Public domain/File:Ford assembly line - 1913.jpg/Wikimedia Commons, 47; AP Images, 49; Supergenijalac/Shutterstock.com, 56; Garsya/iStockphoto.com, 58; Alfred Eisenstaedt/The LIFE Picture Collection/Getty Images, 59; Kaczor58/Shutterstock.com, 63; Henri Docquin/File:Velo Michaux 1861.jpg/Wikimedia Commons, 65; Mary Evans Picture Library, 66; Public domain/File:Pierre Lallemant 1870.jpg/Wikimedia Commons, 70; Patrick Foto/Shutterstock.com, 73; Public Domain/Library of Congress/File:Jos. de Montgolfier, chevalier de l'ordre de St. Michel, inventeur de l'art aérostatique LCCN2002724848.tif/Wikimedia Commons (left), Public Domain/Library of Congress/File:A Etienne de Montgolfier, cooperateur et inventeur de l'art aérostatique LCCN2002724849.tif/Wikimedia Commons (right), 74; Public domain/Vitold Muratov/File:Zeppelin above Leningrad.jpg/Wikimedia Commons, 78; Gerrit de Vries/Shutterstock.com, 80; Tarker/Bridgeman Images, 81; SSPL/Getty Images, 83; Maridav/iStockphoto.com, 89; Darlene Prois/MCT/Newscom, 90; Jupiterimages/Thinkstock, 93; Aragami12345s/Shutterstock.com, 95; NYPL/Science Source/Getty Images, 96; Library of Congress, 103; Rischgitz/Hulton Archive/Getty Images, 104; Albert Pego/Shutterstock.com, 109; Public Domain/US Navy/File:SPS-67 screen.jpg/Wikimedia Commons, 111; Anthony Camerano/AP Images, 112; Sterling, Virginia WSFO/NOAA/File:Wea04086 - Flickr - NOAA Photo Library.jpg/Wikimedia Commons, 116; Rorem/Shutterstock.com, 118; Public domain/William J. Simmons/File:Woodsgr.jpg/Wikimedia Commons, 119; IM_photo/Shutterstock.com, 124; SSPL/Getty Images, 126; Public Domain/John T. Daniels/Library of Congress/File:First flight3.jpg/Wikimedia Commons, 132.

Printed in the United States of America

Contents

Introduction to Transportation Technology

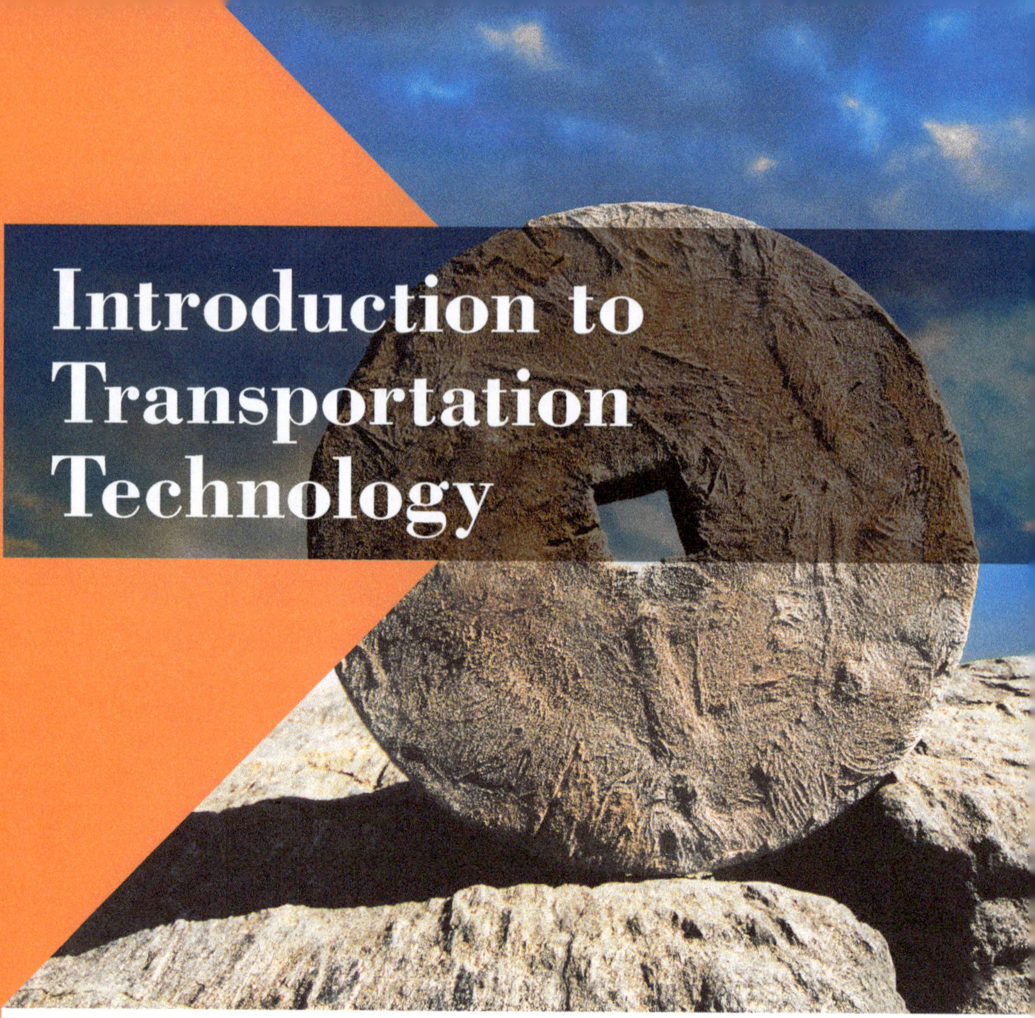

Today, people take many different **modes** of transportation—trains, airplanes, cars, horses—but not many people question where these methods of moving originated, or when. Humanity has evolved over many millennia, and along the way people have invented key elements that enabled them to navigate the world. From around 3500 BCE to the present day, inventions such as the wheel, chariot, and car transported people and goods from one place to another. Today, people continue to invent new and exciting ways to move around, incorporating many inventions that came before into design and concept. Here are a few amazing inventions from around the world, developing over centuries.

Novelties of Transportation

The hectic modern movement of people and goods would seem extraordinary to prehistoric peoples, who mostly traveled on foot, carrying loads in their arms, on their backs, or slung from poles between them. Prehistoric peoples tended to locate their settlements near rivers or coasts. Long-distance travel was done mostly by water, using rafts, boats made from skin and bark, and dugout canoes. Around 7000 BCE, the most sophisticated piece of transportation technology was the sled, dragged by humans. Native American tribes invented the A-shaped *travois*, a large animal skin tied to two long wooden poles that was fastened to either side of an animal and dragged on the ground behind the animal; however, the era of its invention is uncertain. Archaeologists believe human societies first began using animals to pull loads between 5000 and 3000 BCE. Such animals became known as beasts of burden, the "engines" of primitive transportation. The wheel was one of the later developments in prehistoric times, invented around 3500 BCE in the Middle East. By 3000 BCE, wagons and sailing vessels were in common use.

Around 3000 BCE, sailing vessels became increasingly sophisticated, developed by the ancient Egyptians, Minoans, and Phoenicians of the Mediterranean region. The Egyptians were pioneers in ship construction; instead of digging small boats out of trees, they fastened planks onto trees and built upward. The Phoenicians made some of the first sturdy oceangoing ships. The ancient Greeks, who became the dominant civilization in that region around 400 BCE, developed huge, swift ships powered by sails and dozens of oarsmen. Like the Greeks, the Romans (whose empire lasted between 27 BCE and 495 CE) used enormous ships to **ferry** goods around the territories they had conquered in what is now Europe and the Near East. They also developed their ships into formidable weapons of war.

Land transportation also advanced. In Asia, the Chinese and the Persians began constructing the first primitive dirt-track roads between major settlements between around 1000 and 500 BCE. The Romans constructed the world's first network of highways using gravel and stone. Some of these roads, widened and paved, still exist as modern highways.

Water Vessels

Ships became more sophisticated during the Middle Ages in Europe (which lasted from the fall of the Roman Empire to about 1500). They were sturdy and spacious, and they moved faster with more oarsmen and larger areas of sail. These advances allowed Christopher Columbus, Vasco da Gama, and Ferdinand Magellan to make ocean voyages during the fifteenth and sixteenth centuries. Navigation also improved. The Chinese invented the most important navigational device, the magnetic compass, around 1200. In 1537, a Belgian mapmaker named Gerardus Mercator (1512–1594) revolutionized navigation when he developed the **Mercator projection**.

A revolution in shipping began in the eighteenth century when inventors started to explore ways of powering boats using coal-fired **steam engines**. The first steamboat was launched in 1787 by American inventor John Fitch (1743–1798). It was approximately 45 feet (14 meters) long and sailed up the Delaware River at about 6 miles per hour (10 kilometers per hour). Some years later, another

An illustration of the *Clermont* in Albany, New York, circa 1807

American inventor, Robert Fulton (1765–1815), developed a more practical and efficient steamboat. On August 18, 1807, his 150-foot (46 m) steamboat, *Clermont*, made a 300-mile (483 km) round-trip from New York City to Albany in sixty-two hours.

These vessels demonstrated that steam was a practical source of power for ships and boats. Just over a decade after Robert Fulton's voyage, in 1819, the steamship *Savannah* crossed the Atlantic from Savannah, Georgia, to Liverpool, England, in twenty-nine days. However, other inventions were necessary to make great nineteenth-century steamships a reality. One was the iron hull, the basic metal framework of a ship. Another important advance, the screw propeller, was developed by American inventor John Ericsson (1803–1899) and first used in 1844. During the eighteenth century, daring engineers such as Isambard Kingdom Brunel (1806–1859) built enormous transatlantic steamships that could cross the Atlantic Ocean in about two weeks. The biggest of them all, Brunel's *Great Eastern*, completed in 1858, was almost 700 feet (213 m) long, had smokestacks 100 feet (30 m) high, and carried four thousand passengers. Iron ships later gave way to ships made from steel. This stronger and more **versatile** material was developed in the mid-nineteenth century by English inventor Henry Bessemer (1813–1898).

New Ways of Transport

Most people's first experience with steam energy came not from ships but from steam engines on land. The first practical steam engine was developed in 1705 by English engineer Thomas Newcomen (1663–1729) and was originally intended for pumping wastewater out of mines. Within a few decades, other inventors had tried using steam engines to drive vehicles, but the technology was not advanced enough for these attempts to be successful. Around 1770, a French army engineer, Nicolas-Joseph Cugnot (1725–1804), invented the world's first self-propelled road vehicle: a steam-driven automobile-tractor. Although it moved slowly (top speed was 2 mph, or 3.2 kmh), it was not readily maneuverable; when it crashed into a wall and overturned, it was consigned to history.

A breakthrough came in the late eighteenth century when English engineer Richard Trevithick (1771–1833) developed more compact high-pressure steam engines. At the dawn of the nineteenth century, on Christmas Eve of 1801, Trevithick completed the first steam-powered vehicle that could carry passengers; three years later, he built a crude steam locomotive. Twenty more years passed before another English engineer, George Stephenson (1781–1848), made the first practical railroad locomotive. In 1825, the Stockton to Darlington Railway near Newcastle, England, began the world's first steam railroad using Stephenson's engine. The design of steam locomotives improved gradually through the following decades, with innovations being made by many different engineers. In 1872, Canadian-born engineer Elijah McCoy (ca. 1843–1929) invented a way of lubricating (oiling) the moving parts in steam engines automatically, thus

At What Cost?

Transportation lies at the heart of modern society and is equally crucial to national economies. Diesel and **jet engines** power the trucks, locomotives, ships, and planes that carry goods across oceans and continents by land, sea, and air. Inventions such as these, combined with improvements in communications technology, have made it possible for companies to operate effectively in more than one country. During the twentieth century, international transportation became so inexpensive, rapid, and well organized that it was often cheaper for multinational companies to manufacture goods abroad and import them than to manufacture them at home. Similarly, inexpensive transportation has opened up new export markets. Globalization, as these and similar trends have become known, has led to dramatic social changes. Many manufacturing industries have relocated to Asian countries such as China.

Greater use of transportation has come at a price, however. Environmental problems such as smog pollution and global warming are related to the burning of **fossil fuels** in many millions of car, permitting them to run faster and more reliably. Granville Woods (1856–1910) was a developer of electric railroads.

The railroads spread rapidly during the nineteenth century not just because of better locomotives. Ingenious feats of engineering and thousands of workers helped to lay many miles of track over plains; through, around, and over mountain ranges; and across deep valleys. In the United States, one pioneer of this work was German-born American engineer John Roebling (1806–1869), inventor of the suspension bridge. In England, during the 1830s, Isambard Kingdom Brunel made his reputation as the engineer of Britain's Great Western Railway, a railroad that ran hundreds of miles from London, the English capital, to Cornwall, on the southwest coast. The Baltimore and Ohio Railroad became the first railroad in the United States when construction began in 1828. During the second half of the nineteenth century, railroad tracks were laid across the entire North American continent. The first transcontinental railroad was completed in Utah

truck, ship, and airplane engines. Much of the world's oil is supplied by countries of the Middle East, a politically unstable region of the world. So many vehicles are now on the move that traffic congestion has itself become a major environmental and economic problem.

Although globalization has brought many companies greater wealth and many individuals a greater choice of affordable goods, some people believe it has undermined jobs in Western countries and encouraged environmental pollution and sweatshops in developing nations. The transportation of goods and people has grown enormously since the twentieth century, but that growth cannot continue to be sustained by the earth. Some people believe the solution to these problems may be to reduce the need for travel by using advanced communications technologies such as the Internet. Others think environmentally friendly cars, trucks, ships, and planes may address the problem. One thing is certain: inventors are sure to discover better forms of transportation in the future.

on May 10, 1869. By 1930, when the railroad network reached its peak, 430,000 miles (692,018 km) of track had been laid, enough to stretch from New York City to Los Angeles 175 times.

From Rail to Road

Railroads revolutionized long-distance transportation and played an important part in making western states accessible to settlers. However, trains could visit only those places where there was track and, despite the efforts of engineers such as Cugnot and Trevithick, steam-driven road vehicles never became popular. For shorter distances and more local journeys, the horse remained the most important form of transportation until the end of the nineteenth century.

Human power offered one solution to the problem of local travel in the form of the bicycle. An early, primitive bicycle, called the **draisine** or the dandyhorse, was patented by German tax collector Karl von Drais (1785–1851) in 1818. Instead of pedaling, the cyclist simply straddled the frame and ran along. A better design, credited to French inventor Pierre Michaux (1813–1883) and others, appeared in the 1860s. Michaux's "boneshaker" was aptly named; its iron and wooden wheels had no suspension and offered a most uncomfortable ride, but it was propelled by pedaling and was thus faster than the dandyhorse. As bicycles became popular, they became faster and more comfortable. Rubber tires first appeared around the 1870s, greatly increasing demand for a tougher kind of "vulcanized" rubber that had been developed in 1839 by American inventor Charles Goodyear (1800–1860).

Bicycles were versatile and affordable, but how far and how fast riders could pedal were limited, as was the amount and weight of goods a bicycle could carry. A more compact source of power than the steam engine was needed. Steam engines worked by an external combustion process. An open-air fire burned coal, which heated water in a boiler to make steam. The expanding steam pushed a **piston** back and forth in a large metal cylinder (like a bicycle pump moving in and out) to produce power and motion. In the seventeenth century, Christiaan Huygens (1629–1695), a Dutch physicist, realized that burning the fuel inside the cylinder would be more efficient. He came up with the idea of internal combustion. Another two centuries were to pass, however, before this idea would become one of the most important inventions of all time: the gasoline engine.

Numerous inventors played a part in the development of the gasoline engine, beginning in 1860 with French engineer Joseph Étienne Lenoir (1822–1900). Seven years later, German engineer Nikolaus August Otto (1832–1891) developed an efficient gasoline engine. It was the first real mechanical alternative to inefficient steam engines. In the last few years of the nineteenth century, another German engineer, Rudolf Diesel (1858–1913), developed a simple, powerful engine that could run on almost any fuel. More robust than the gasoline engine, the diesel engine was soon used in factories, ships, power plants, trucks, submarines, and automobiles.

The smaller gasoline engine led to more compact, personal forms of transportation in the second half of the nineteenth century. One of the first to explore this area was German engineer Karl Benz (1844–1929), who built his own gasoline engine in 1878. By 1885, he had fastened this machine to a three-wheeled bicycle carriage and produced the Tri-Car—which many people regard as the world's first gasoline-powered automobile. His rival, Gottlieb Daimler (1834–1900), then produced a four-wheeled car. Together, Daimler and Benz ushered in the age of modern motoring. American industrialist Henry Ford (1863–1947) introduced his Model T in 1908. Significantly, Ford developed the **assembly line** for his factories; this form of manufacturing allowed him to make cars in greater quantity with less expense; thus he could charge less for his automobiles and more people could afford them. Japanese industrialist Soichiro Honda (1906–1991) performed a similar feat with the motorcycle.

The first cars were basic: Benz's Tri-Car had no roof to protect against the rain, and the engine in Ford's Model T had to be started by a hand crank. Later inventors turned their ingenuity to making cars more automated and refined. Charles Kettering (1876–1958) developed the electric ignition (a car's automated starting system, which replaced the hand crank), and Mary Anderson (1866–1953) invented windshield wipers. Others made driving cars safer, including Garrett Morgan (1877–1963), who developed traffic signals, and Allen Breed (1927–1999), who invented the air bag.

To the Sky

Archaeologists believe ancient civilizations experimented with flight, but not until 1783 were human dreams of flying realized. That year, French brothers Joseph-Michel Montgolfier (1740–1810) and Jacques-Étienne Montgolfier (1745–1799) flew the first hot air balloons. Simple spherical balloons had no means of control and blew wherever the wind took them, so they were more of a novelty than a practical form of transportation. By 1900, however, a German inventor named Ferdinand von Zeppelin (1838–1917) had developed a better design: a lozenge-shaped balloon, built around a metal framework, powered by engines with propellers. This conveyance could be steered and directed. Named after their inventor, zeppelins were known as airships and could fly for days at a time. However, they were soon superseded by a better form of air travel.

Most innovators in transportation developed their revolutionary ideas by studying earlier inventions and determining how to improve them. Karl Benz used a bicycle carriage to form his first car, and

The world became more accessible with the invention of engine-powered transport, such as the airplane.

Henry Ford was inspired by a steam tractor he saw on his family's farm. Two of the greatest aerospace innovators were similarly inspired. Orville Wright (1871–1948) and Wilbur Wright (1867–1912) began as bicycle makers in a machine shop in Dayton, Ohio, and took their ideas from gliders (unpowered aircraft). In December 1903, they too surpassed the inventions that had ignited their imaginations when they became the first to fly an engine-powered airplane. The Wrights, in turn, prompted other inventors to devise better airplanes. One, a Russian-born engineer named Igor Sikorsky (1889–1972), met Wilbur Wright in 1908 and then decided to make an aircraft that could fly to places airplanes could not. He finally realized his ambition in 1943, during World War II, when the world's first practical helicopter went into production.

The modern airplane jet engine was born just before World War II as a result of a rivalry between Englishman Frank Whittle (1907–1996) and German Hans Pabst von Ohain (1911–1998): Whittle developed the first engine, but Ohain made the first flight. Once the potential of jet airplanes was realized, engineers were soon making them fly farther and faster. Jet planes became rocket planes, and during the 1950s humans began the conquest of space. Space travel seems a natural evolution from air travel, yet the invention of space rockets predated jet engines by more than a decade. The first space rocket was actually launched in 1926, from a cabbage patch on a farm in Auburn, Massachusetts, by American physicist Robert H. Goddard (1882–1945). Goddard did not live to see astronauts blasting into space or reaching the moon in 1969, but these achievements would not have been possible without him.

Each new century has yielded different transportation inventions that have either built on existing inventions or been established as standalone products or **prototypes**. Today there are many ways to get around, and new ways are being developed, but it is clear that without inventions from those people before, society would not be what it is today.

Inventor of the Windshield Wiper

Mary Anderson

1866–1953

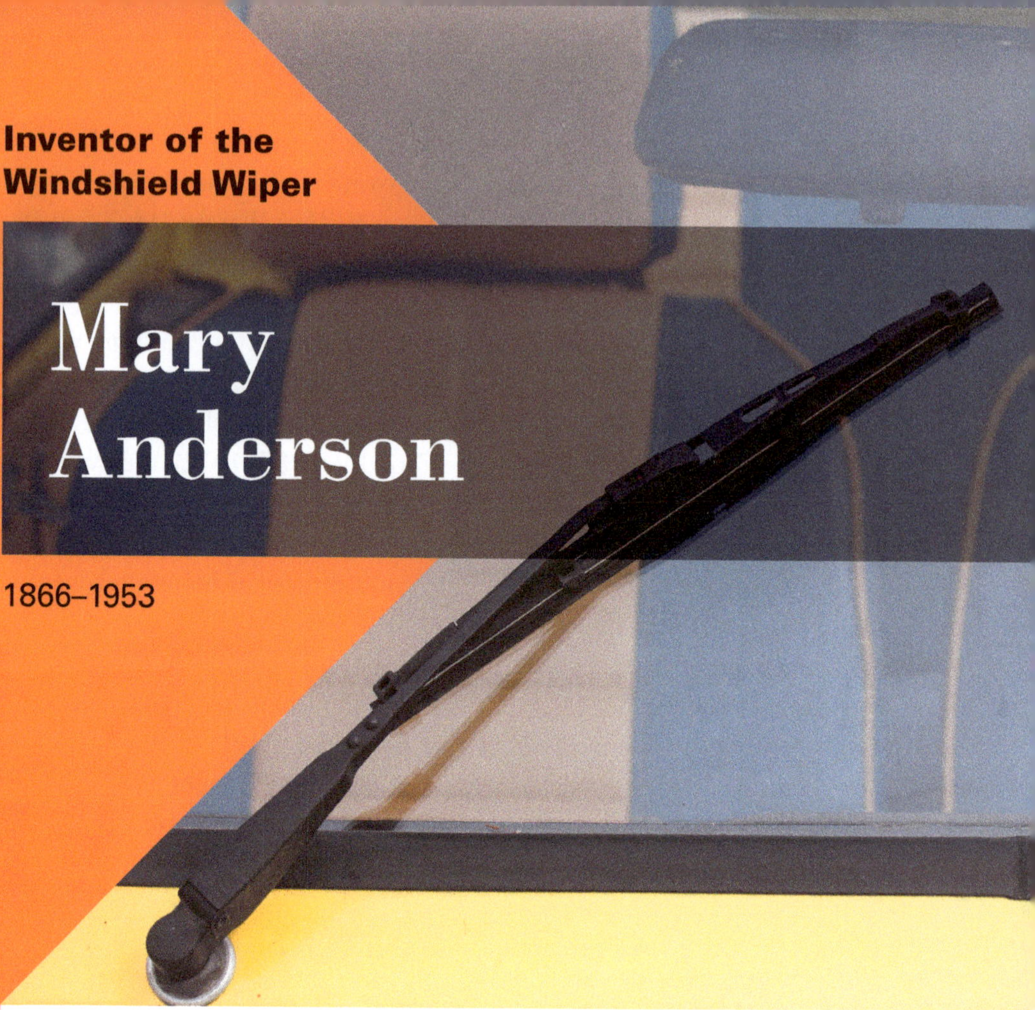

Sometimes inventions become so much a part of a different invention that one would assume the two have always gone together. However, that is not always the case. Take, for example, the windshield wiper. Today, windshield wipers are on every car on the road, and many would think that the car and windshield wiper were invented together; however, it was not until the twentieth century that the first windshield wipers came into being. The woman who created them was Mary Anderson. She lived during a time when there were few women inventors, and even fewer who had invented products that would truly change the way society functioned.

Beginning Years

Very little biographical information exists about Mary Anderson, other than that she was from Birmingham, Alabama, and was born in 1866. Some accounts refer to her as a Southern belle, but it is unclear whether she was married or single, and whether she had an occupation. Written accounts of her life focus almost solely on a winter trip she took to New York City in 1903.

Defining the Problem

Anderson dreamed up the windshield wiper while riding in New York City streetcars. She noticed that the streetcar drivers had to stop frequently to clear snow or ice by hand from the windshield. In rainy or misty weather, drivers would often have to open windows and stick their heads out to see. Such stops and starts made travel unnecessarily slow and unsafe for both driver and passengers. So, Anderson began to draw a solution to the problem in her sketchbook.

Designing the Solution

Anderson drew a spring-loaded arm with a rubber blade that could clear debris, such as rain, sleet, snow, mud, or even dust, from a windshield. It would be operated by hand from inside the car, via a mechanical lever. The spring-loaded arm attached to the lever would swing the blade across the window and back into its original position. Thus, drivers would not have to leave the wheel or stop their vehicles to see. Her invention would make driving easier, more comfortable, and safer.

Applying the Solution

Back home in Alabama, Anderson found that few people would take her idea seriously. Many thought her safety device would actually distract or "hypnotize" drivers and cause accidents. The same has been said of many newer technologies, such as the car radio. However, Anderson persevered, and in 1904 she applied for a patent. The following year she was awarded US Patent No. 743,801 for her spring-loaded windshield wiper.

Unfortunately, Anderson was unsuccessful selling her device to car manufacturers. At the time, there was not a pressing need; many of the earliest automobiles had no windshield because they did not go fast enough to need one. Moreover, in areas outside major cities, few people owned cars. Most people still relied on horse-drawn buggies, carriages, or wagons for transportation. As far as historians can determine, Anderson set the patent aside and it eventually expired.

Mary Anderson

A decade later, however, advances in automobile manufacture opened the door to the windshield wiper's success. The Model T, first built by Henry Ford in 1908, revolutionized American automobile culture because the middle class could afford to buy cars. As car design evolved and enclosed compartments became more common, the need for windshield wipers grew.

The Tri-Continental Corporation (Trico), founded in Buffalo, New York, was one of the first companies to successfully market a windshield-wiping device. The wiper was created by the company's founder, J. R. Oishei, in 1917, after he accidentally drove his car into a bicyclist on a rainy night. Oishei's invention was tailored to the split-window windshields of the early twentieth century. His wipers were a success, and, in fact, Trico still manufactures wipers. Oishei apparently developed his wipers independently of Mary Anderson's work.

The same year Oishei founded Trico, Charlotte Bridgwood received a patent for the first automatic windshield wiper, called the "Storm Windshield Cleaner." Bridgwood's invention relied on rollers instead of a rubber blade. However, her device, like Anderson's, was not a commercial success.

The Impact of the Solution on Society

Windshield wipers became truly widespread in the 1940s and 1950s, as technological advances made them more powerful and useful.

Two-speed wipers arrived in the late 1940s, and Robert Kearns (1928–2005) created intermittent wipers in 1967. His design, which had variable speeds, was a great advance on previous electrical wipers. The most recent improvements on Mary Anderson's invention include moisture-sensing wipers that automatically turn themselves on at the correct speed. Wipers themselves can now be found on every windshield, some car headlights, airplanes, and even space shuttles.

Despite her achievements, more than a century after her invention was created, Mary Anderson remains a mostly anonymous inventor.

Making Cars Safe

Early cars were not always built with safety in mind. However, as cars began to travel at higher speeds, and as car ownership increased in the United States, safety devices proliferated.

Anderson invented her windshield wiper in the first days of concern about the safety of automobiles, the early 1900s. Other notable safety inventions from this early period included safety glass—reinforced glass that was less likely to shatter, invented in 1903—and electric turn signals, invented in 1907.

Safety did not become a significant priority until the 1950s. That decade saw four-wheel disc brakes introduced, as well as the first cars with seat belts. Crumple zones—parts of the car designed to absorb the impact of collisions—were first used by Mercedes-Benz in 1953. In 1959, Volvo introduced the three-point seat belt, which is now a standard safety device in cars. Air bags, first patented in 1968 by Allen Breed, were introduced as a safety option in 1974 but did not become standard until the 1990s. Antilock brakes were introduced in 1991.

In the twenty-first century, automobile safety has seen even more advances. Computers and cutting-edge technologies such as dynamic steering response (which corrects steering according to road conditions) not only help keep drivers and passengers safe in the event of accidents but also help prevent accidents. As years progress, car manufacturers now keep safety at the forefront of their minds when designing new vehicles for the roads.

The Trico plant in Buffalo, New York, where J. R. Oishei invented and manufactured a popular version of windshield wipers in 1917

Today her contributions are noted and admired, and slowly she is beginning to regain recognition in the automotive industry. She is a testament of the difficulties women inventors faced in early times and a role model for other inventors that shows they, too, can change the world with a small sketch and ambition.

Timeline

1866
Mary Anderson born

1903
Anderson's visit to New York City inspires her invention

1904
Anderson receives a patent for the windshield wiper

1917
J. R. Oishei of the Tri-Continental Corporation also invents a windshield wiper

1953
Anderson dies

Inventor of the Gasoline Automobile

Karl Benz

1844–1929

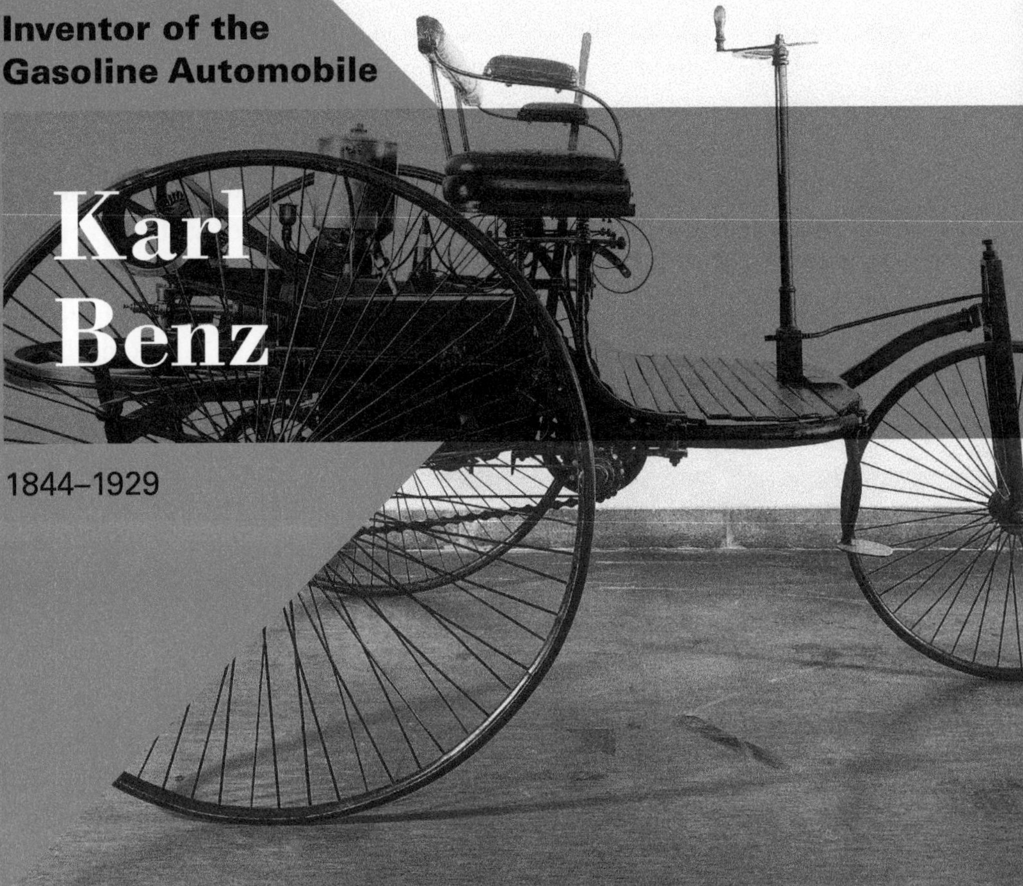

Not all inventors set out to create something that will change the world. Many invent products that interest them, and only later is the novelty and importance of their product realized and adopted by society. Such is the case of Karl Benz. Benz invented the first gasoline-powered car in 1885, but despite its innovation, it did not have immediate success in the marketplace. However, today in the twenty-first century, Benz's automobile has become the most important invention in modern times.

Dawn of the Inventor

When Karl Benz was born in Karlsruhe, Germany, on November 25, 1844, there was not a single gas-powered car anywhere on the planet. People traveled by horse or bicycle, or on foot; for longer journeys, they might have taken a train or a boat.

Benz's father, Johann George Benz, was a locomotive driver who died in a railroad accident when Karl was only two years old. His mother, Josephine Vaillant, raised him on her own. His formal education began in 1853, when he was nine years old, at the Lyzeum scientific school in Karlsruhe. Later, Benz attended high school, then moved to the Karlsruhe Polytechnic, before completing his education at a technical college. Although he had intended to be a locksmith, he graduated as a mechanical engineer on July 9, 1864.

Car Adventures

Karl Benz is often called the inventor of the automobile, but in reality many different individuals' work led to its creation. As early as 1769, Frenchman Nicolas-Joseph Cugnot (1725–1804) had built a gigantic steam-driven tractor that was arguably the world's first primitive automobile. Unlike a modern car, it was powered by a coal fire that boiled water to make steam. The steam pushed a piston in and out of a metal cylinder, like a large bicycle pump, using this back-and-forth motion to make the wheels rotate. Steam engines like these were designated external combustion engines because the coal burned (was combusted) outside (external to) the cylinder where the power was produced. They wasted a great deal of heat; huge amounts of coal were needed to travel even short distances.

During the nineteenth century, various inventors tried to develop compact engines that used fuels more convenient than coal. Such engines were known as internal combustion engines because they burned the fuel inside (internal to) the cylinders where the power was produced. The first practical engine of this kind was built in 1860 by a Frenchman named Joseph Étienne Lenoir (1822–1900) and was powered by the gas that was used in streetlights. Several years later, German engineer Nikolaus Otto (1832–1891) developed a better engine that generated power by burning fuel in a series of four steps that repeated endlessly, known as the Otto cycle.

Over the next six years, he worked for various engineering companies, beginning as a **draftsman** and later becoming an engineering designer and manager. In 1871, at age twenty-seven, he joined forces with another engineer, August Ritter, to set up an engineering company named the Iron Foundry and Mechanical Workshop. It specialized in supplying construction materials to other engineering firms.

Karl Benz and his wife, Bertha, in 1894

Around this time, Benz had begun courting his future wife, the optimistic and independent Bertha Ringer (1849–1944). Her first demonstration of loyalty to Benz came before they were married. August Ritter was proving to be an erratic and unsuitable business partner. When the engineering firm almost went bankrupt, less than one year after opening, Bertha offered Karl her bridal dowry as a way of settling the firm's debts and buying out Ritter.

Defining the Problem

Karl Benz and Bertha were married on July 20, 1872. It was the start of a new life for the young engineer, and he began to consider better ways of making money. Like many, he relied on a bicycle for getting around, but pedaling was hard work and he wondered if he could invent a better mode of transportation.

Designing the Solution

During the 1870s, Karl Benz began tinkering with engines. He started by studying Nikolaus Otto's invention and tried to make a gasoline engine that worked in two steps instead of four. He finally achieved this "two-stroke" engine on December 31, 1878, patenting the machine shortly afterward.

Once his engine was ready to manufacture, he sought investors to help set up a factory. With his wife's enthusiastic backing and financial support from several other partners, he formed a company, Gasmotoren Fabrik Mannheim, in 1882. However, he had to sell so much stock in the company to raise money that he was left with only a 5 percent share and little control over what the company did. When the other partners took over the job of designing engines, Benz quit the firm only one year after its founding.

A few months later, Benz found two sympathetic new backers, Max Rose and Friedrich Wilhelm Esslinger. With their help, he established a new company, Benz & Co., to manufacture his engines. The company grew rapidly and soon had twenty-five employees. Now Benz was able to turn his attention to a new challenge: transforming his engine into a complete automobile.

Facing Problems and Solutions

Karl Benz had to solve three problems when he invented the first automobile in 1888. First, he needed a reliable source of power. This came from the compact gasoline engine that he had developed several years earlier. Second, he had to make some sort of carriage to hold passengers and their goods. Benz constructed a simple chassis with two large wheels at the back; a single, smaller wheel at the front for steering; and a flat platform in between. The three-wheel arrangement gave the vehicle its familiar name: the Tri-Car.

The third problem for Benz was making the engine and the carriage work together. Gottlieb Daimler had created his car simply by mounting his gasoline engine on an existing horse-drawn carriage. Benz was more innovative, however, because he designed not just the engine and the carriage but various extra pieces of technology to make the engine power the carriage successfully. Thus, he designed the clutch and gearshift system (to make the car use more or less power for different driving conditions), and the accelerator (to make

Inventors often modify existing inventions to produce something that is partly old and partly new. Karl Benz was no exception. The machine he produced in 1885 is often described as the world's first car, as though it were a completely original invention. In fact, it was a combination of Benz's existing gasoline engine, itself based on Nikolaus Otto's work, and a carriage-contraption that looked like a three-wheeled bicycle.

Benz was not the only person working to invent an automobile. Another German engineer, Gottlieb Daimler (1834–1900), had designed a gasoline-driven engine in 1885 and was also trying to develop a car. Although Benz and Daimler later became rivals, historians do not believe they knew of one another's work initially. As is often the case in the history of invention, when one technology develops to a certain point, several inventors think of the same idea at almost exactly the same time. It was luck, more than anything else, that led to Benz having achieved success before Daimler.

it go faster or slower). To carry power from the engine to the wheels, he invented a special differential gear. This device rotated the drive shaft that carried power from the engine through 90 degrees so that it could turn the rear wheels. He also invented the carburetor, which mixed air and fuel in the engine, and the sparking plug, which set the air-fuel mixture alight and generated power.

By the standard of a modern car, Benz's vehicle was primitive. Power came from a 0.75-horsepower, one-cylinder engine that produced a top speed of 10 miles per hour (16 kmh). Moreover, Benz's car had no steering wheel; instead, a simple lever turned the front wheel to the left or right. Levers also controlled the gearshift and the brakes. The Tri-Car was difficult to control, and on his first outing, Benz crashed it into a wall. Yet what the car lacked in refinements it more than made up for with innovation, and it proved that the basic concept of the car was a good one.

Applying the Solution

Benz secured his invention with a patent, granted on January 29, 1886—but the modern motorcar was not born, fully formed, at that moment. To begin with, no one was interested in Benz's odd-looking three-wheeled motor carriage. The business began to take off only two years later, thanks to the help of the spirited Bertha Benz. On August 5, 1888, she borrowed her husband's new car and set off on a 65-mile (105 km) journey to visit her mother. The trip took the whole day, partly because there were no gas stations at that time; instead, she had to stop to refuel at drugstores (where gasoline could then be bought). When she arrived, she sent a telegram to her husband and told him what she had done. Helpfully, she reported that the car was impossible to drive uphill unless the passengers got out and pushed; this information prompted Benz to add better **gears**. News of the epic journey soon caught the public's imagination and helped to increase interest in the car.

Even so, Benz's tiny three-wheeler never sold especially well. Highways were nonexistent; most roads were little more than two-wheeled tracks made by horses and carts. Benz's three-wheeled car had great difficulty on such roads because there was no rut for the central steering wheel to rest in. Benz's rival, Gottlieb Daimler, was already building four-wheeled cars that could use the primitive roads more successfully. In 1893, Benz was forced to follow suit. His first four-wheeled car, the Viktoria, was a greater success: despite a price of $4,500 (equivalent to about $110,000 US in 2014), he sold forty-five cars that year. The following year, he introduced an even better automobile, the Velo, manufacturing approximately 1,200 vehicles of this design.

The Impact of the Solution on Society

As the twentieth century began, Benz was the world's most successful carmaker, but he was not alone. He was facing increasing competition from other manufacturers, notably Daimler, whose Mercedes cars were better designed, faster, and more innovative. Benz refused to concede that Daimler was making better cars, but as the competition mounted

Today, the Mercedes car company is recognized by its logo.

he had to respond. In 1903, he developed a car, the Parsifil, with a top speed of 37 miles per hour (60 kmh), which he hoped would beat Daimler. When this move failed, some of the directors of the Benz Company decided to hire a new car designer. Although they did not actually tell Benz, he soon found out. He decided to resign as head of his own company. His two sons, Richard and Eugen, who helped him in the firm, left too. Benz remained on the board but also set up a new firm named Benz Söhne, which he established in 1906 with his sons.

In 1904, Richard Benz returned to the Benz Company, where he worked as a car designer and factory manager. Over the next few years, the company's fortunes were restored. The intense rivalry between Benz and Daimler continued until 1926, when the two companies merged, forming a single firm named Daimler-Benz AG. During the twentieth century, the company earned a reputation for its prestigious Mercedes-Benz automobiles. In 1998, it merged with the US-based Chrysler Corporation to form the car manufacturer Daimler-Chrysler.

Karl Benz spent the final years of his life with his wife in a large house beside the Neckar River in the town of Ladenburg, Germany. It was no conventional home; it had a large garage built into it and a machine shop where Benz continued to tinker with new car designs.

He extended and improved the house several times over the years, and it was there that he died on April 4, 1929, at age eighty-four. Today, the house is a museum dedicated to Karl Benz's life and work.

During his lifetime, Benz was able to see the effect his invention and other similar ones that came after it had on society. There is no doubt that Benz, along with his contemporaries, changed the way people transported themselves and their goods around the world. Today, the automobile industry is one of the largest industries on Earth. Vehicles exist in all countries, and more and more people own cars each year. It is clear that Benz helped revolutionize the world with his gasoline-powered automobile, and society has relied heavily on his concept ever since.

Timeline

1844
Karl Benz born in Karlsruhe, Germany

1864
Benz graduates from technical college as a mechanical engineer

1871
Benz sets up the Iron Foundry and Mechanical Workshop with August Ritter

1879
Benz patents the two-stroke gasoline engine

1883
Benz founds Benz & Co. to manufacture his engines

1886
Benz receives a patent for his three-wheeled motor carriage

1893
Benz introduces his first four-wheeled car, the Viktoria

1903
Benz resigns as head of the Benz Company

1906
Benz establishes Benz Söhne with his sons

1929
Benz dies

Inventor of the Air Bag

Allen Breed

1927–1999

Prior to the 1960s, the car was a vehicle that transported people to and from places, but it had very few mechanisms to keep passengers safe. One of the first products created with the intention of saving passengers' lives was the air bag. Inventor Allen Breed faced difficulties getting his invention recognized, but eventually he triumphed. Today the air bag is a central feature in any car, essential to protecting passengers when needed.

Starting Out

Breed was born and raised in Chicago in 1927, the son of a doctor who pioneered radiation therapy for cancer patients. Although he was expected to follow in his father's footsteps and pursue medicine,

Allen Breed in 1968

Breed showed an early aptitude for engineering. A self-described gadgeteer, he had a knack for takings things apart and putting them back together—cars in particular.

After high school, Breed joined the navy; following World War II, he pursued a mechanical engineering degree at Northwestern University, doubling up on classes and finishing in about half the usual time. His first job after college was with RCA—first in product design and later as a manager of manufacturing and design engineering. In 1957, after a stint with the Gruen Watch Company, Breed founded his first company, Waltham Engineering. He was thirty years old.

Defining the Problem

In 1961, Breed founded another company, Breed Corporation, which developed safety and arming devices for missiles, mines, and artillery shells. His primary customer was the US military.

Among several other devices, Breed Corporation developed sensor triggers—safety-oriented designs that ensured, for instance, that an artillery shell would explode only when deployed, not when a solider dropped it accidentally. Over time, Breed realized that the same devices could be used in automotive safety for inflating air bags.

Designing the Solution

Air bags were not an entirely new concept. They had been utilized in planes in the 1940s, and a rudimentary automotive air bag had been designed in the early 1950s. However, even though American car culture blossomed in the 1960s, no workable, commercially successful design was available.

Breed believed he could fill that void. Existing controlled-explosion technology could be used to rapidly inflate an air bag, but the heart of his invention was a new electromechanical ball-in-tube sensor trigger—a metal ball, normally held in place by magnets, would break free under the sudden force of a collision, completing an electrical circuit and triggering the inflation of the bag. The same technology had been used to trigger the firing of missiles and mines. Breed patented his electromechanical sensor air bag system, the first of its kind, in 1968.

Applying the Solution

America should have been primed for Breed's invention. Consumer-rights advocate Ralph Nader had published a scathing report on the state of automotive safety, *Unsafe at Any Speed*, in 1965. President Lyndon B. Johnson had recently signed into law the 1966 National Traffic and Motor Vehicle Safety Act. Still, for more than fifteen years, Breed and his air bag technology were met with rejection after rejection.

Breed was determined, however. He testified before Congress about the benefits of air bags and worked tirelessly to convince the top US automakers—those known as the big three: General Motors (GM), Chrysler, and Ford—to adopt his safety technology. From 1969 to 1984, Breed carried a copy of the latest version of his air bag technology in his pocket—a testimony to his perseverance.

During that time, US automakers toyed with airbag technology. In 1971, GM installed air bags on a government-only model of Chevrolet. In 1973, air bags were an option in the Oldsmobile Toronado and some types of Chevrolets. By the mid-1970s, air bags could be found in full-size Oldsmobiles and Buicks. Overall, however, the product did not have much commercial success. Few customers were willing to spend money on an optional safety device. Then, in July 1984, the federal government announced it would require that all new cars have driver-side air bags or automatic seat belts within five years. Breed's company was one of only two air bag manufacturers in the world.

Growth was explosive. By 1987, one in ten cars had air bags. In 1988, one-quarter of cars had them. The following year, almost half of cars had air bags. In 1990, more than twenty years after Breed had invented the technology, driver-side air bags were finally standard issue on all US cars. In 1991, Congress passed yet another mandate: all new passenger vehicles should be equipped with driver-side and passenger-side air bags by 1998.

All these federal regulations resulted in a 30 to 50 percent decline in automotive fatalities and serious injuries. The regulations also guaranteed astronomical financial growth for Breed's company, renamed Breed Technologies. The company made its debut on the stock market in 1993. That year, sales were more than $150 million.

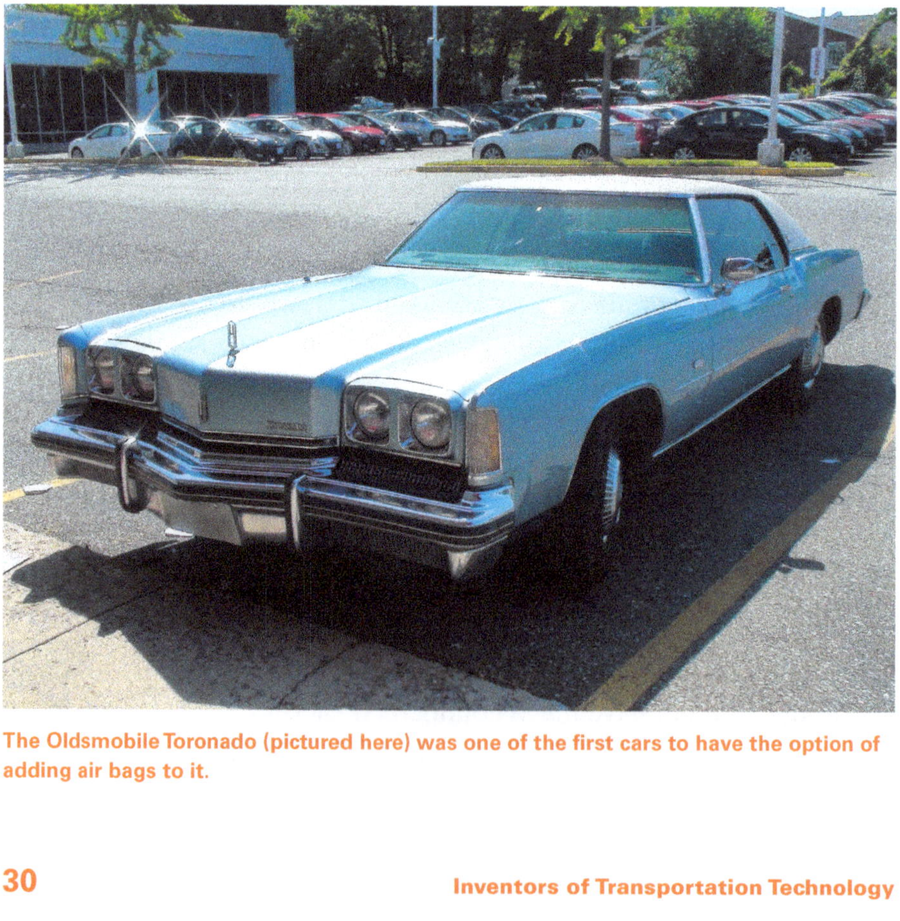

The Oldsmobile Toronado (pictured here) was one of the first cars to have the option of adding air bags to it.

Breed Technologies enjoyed continued success throughout the early 1990s. However, setbacks occurred. The safety of air bags themselves was called into question when a number of passengers and drivers—primarily women and children—died from air bag impact in low-speed or minor-impact collisions. In Pennsylvania, for instance, an exploding air bag inflicted fatal skull fractures on a newborn in a 25-mile-per-hour (40 kmh) crash.

In response, Breed Technologies and others in the industry patented new technologies to increase air bag safety. As these advances were made, it became clear that electronic sensors were the way of the future, and Breed's patented electromechanical design was being steadily replaced by more high-tech products. To keep up with the market, in 1994, Breed Technologies began purchasing other air bag industry firms to help develop new crash sensors, firing mechanisms, air bags, steering wheels, and seat belts. Many of these acquisitions were financed on credit, and by the late 1990s, the once successful company was saddled with debt.

In 1997, Breed was diagnosed with cancer and stepped down from daily operations of the company. He handed over the reins to Johnnie Breed, his wife of ten years and an accomplished businesswoman.

Breed succumbed to cancer on December 13, 1999, at age seventy-two—a mere two months after he was inducted into the Automotive Hall of Fame. Breed Technologies had filed for Chapter 11 bankruptcy a couple of months earlier. The firm remained under bankruptcy protection until late 2000, when it reemerged as a private company.

For his contributions to automotive safety and his success in the business world, Breed was greatly acclaimed. In addition to being honored by the Automotive Hall of Fame, in 1993 he was elected Florida Entrepreneur of the Year and, in 1995, National Entrepreneur of the Year. In 1996, he was inducted into the Tampa Bay Business Hall of Fame; in 1998, he was named the Ernst & Young Entrepreneur of the Year. In 1999, he received a Lifetime Achievement Award from *Automotive & Transportation Interiors* magazine.

The Impact of the Solution on Society

Since Allen Breed's introduction of his air bag in 1968, technology for the devices has improved greatly. Many modern vehicles have side and window air bags, in addition to front and passenger air bags. Moreover, air bag technology can even sense the weight and height of individuals in the car, and computers can calculate the best angle and force with which to deploy the air bag. Because of Allen Breed's invention, many people's lives have been saved, and today the air bag continues to be a modern safety feature in new automobiles.

Timeline

1927
Allen Breed born in Chicago

1957
Breed founds Waltham Engineering

1961
Breed founds Breed Corporation

1968
Breed patents his air bag system

1984
All new cars are required by law to have driver's side air bags or seat belts within five years

1990
Driver's side air bags are standard on all US cars

1995
Breed named National Entrepreneur of the Year

1999
Breed dies

Pioneer Automobile Manufacturer, Inventor of the Motorcycle

Gottlieb Daimler

1834–1900

Over the years, the automobile industry has grown into one of the world's most massive and influential industries. There were many pioneers in the automobile industry when it first began. One of them was Gottlieb Daimler, who founded Daimler Motor Company. This company sold many cars and continues to do so today as the Daimler-Chrysler company. Daimler's work inspired others, and his legacy lives on as part of the ever-growing world of automobiles.

An Inventor Begins

Gottlieb Wilhelm Daimler was born March 17, 1834, in Schorndorf, Württemberg, Germany. The son of a master baker, Daimler attended technical school from 1848 to 1852, while also

Wilhelm Maybach (*left*) and Gottlieb Daimler (*right*)

apprenticing with a gunsmith in Stuttgart. From 1853 to 1857, he worked in a steam-engine locomotive factory in Strasbourg. He then completed his education at the Stuttgart Polytechnic, in preparation for a career as a mechanical engineer.

After working briefly in Paris, Daimler traveled in England in 1861, working at a variety of engineering plants in Leeds, Manchester, and elsewhere. In 1862, he attended the world's fair in London, where he saw the latest advances in European engineering.

Defining the Problem

Daimler returned to Germany in 1863 and became manager of an engineering workshop in Reutlingen. This facility, known as the Bruderhaus, operated in conjunction with a progressive orphanage designed to provide orphans and other socially disadvantaged children with the opportunity to learn engineering skills. Among the orphans living at the Bruderhaus, Daimler met the teenage Wilhelm Maybach (1846–1926) and immediately recognized that the young man had the potential to become a brilliant engineer. Maybach became Daimler's **protégé**, and the two men would continue to work closely together for the remainder of the century.

In 1869, Daimler brought Maybach with him when he was hired as director of the Maschinenbau Gesellschaft, a factory in Karlsruhe that manufactured locomotives. In 1872, Daimler became chief engineer of another factory, the Deutz Gasmotoren-Fabrik, which produced various types of gas-powered engines, and he made Maybach head of design. At the Deutz factory the two men worked with Nikolaus Otto (1832–1891; one of the owners of the factory), who in 1876 developed the four-stroke engine known as the Otto Atmospheric Engine. Regarded as the best internal combustion engine of its time, the engine was still much too large for practical use in an automobile. Daimler envisioned a lighter engine, capable of reaching high speeds quickly.

Designing the Solution

After attempting to modify Otto's design, Daimler and Maybach left Deutz and set up their own manufacturing plant in Stuttgart in 1882. They were intent on developing light, fast-revving, gasoline-powered engines for use in motor vehicles. At first they encountered difficulties developing a reliable ignition system, but within a year Daimler had invented an ignition device with an incandescent tube in the cylinder head, which he patented in 1883.

Daimler and Maybach had also been occupied with a design for a smaller engine that could be used to power a moving vehicle. Their first experiment in this area led to their creating the world's first authentic motorcycle. In 1885, the two men fitted a small gas-powered engine onto a specially designed wooden bicycle, which Daimler's son Paul rode for some 6 miles (9.6 km) on its first outing. The inventors regarded the motorcycle, however, as merely a test run for more ambitious motorized vehicles.

The following year they fitted a more powerful, one-cylinder, water-cooled engine to a conventional four-wheel carriage. Soon they were attempting to use their engines to power boats, streetcars, and even airships. At the 1889 world's fair in Paris, they exhibited a two-cylinder V-engine mounted in a new four-wheel car frame. This engine contained a carburetor that could inject evaporated gasoline mixed with air for use as the engine's fuel, a four-speed gearbox, and a belt-driven device for turning the wheels. The new vehicle could travel at about 11 miles per hour (17.7 kmh).

Applying the Solution

In 1890, Daimler founded the Daimler Motoren-Gesellschaft (Daimler Motor Company) in Stuttgart. After only one year, both he and Maybach left the company because of disagreements with some of its leading investors, who had begun to take control of its direction. The two men continued to work independently on design ideas for automobiles

The Story of Mercedes

Emil Jellinek (1853–1918) enjoyed a life of high style on the French Riviera at the beginning of the twentieth century. A wealthy diplomat for the Austro-Hungarian Empire who lived in Vienna, Austria, and Nice, France, Jellinek associated with many other wealthy people on the Riviera who wanted the finest, most advanced modern luxuries. An automobile enthusiast who had entered a number of road races in Europe (using his daughter's name, Mercedes, as his racing name),

The Mercedes-Benz was named after the daughter of an automobile enthusiast.

(the other investors wanted the company to focus on the production of stationary engines). Daimler's cars made impressive showings in some of the early road races in Europe—including a victory in the first international auto race, the 1894 Paris-to-Rouen race. Such successes allowed Daimler to resume control of the Daimler Motor Company in 1895. He once again made Maybach his chief engineer.

The Impact of the Solution on Society

After Daimler and Maybach regained control, they entered a period of success, starting with the Mercedes. The car became quite popular

Jellinek knew he would be able to sell the best automobile available to his wealthy friends.

When he approached the Daimler Motor Company to produce such an automobile in 1900, Jellinek offered to purchase thirty-six cars on two conditions: first, he wanted to be the sole agent for the new car throughout the Austro-Hungarian Empire, as well as in France and the United States. Second, he wanted the car to be named after his eleven-year-old daughter, Mercedes. The German name "Daimler," he explained, could hurt the car's sales potential in France. Daimler's longtime partner Wilhelm Maybach, along with Daimler's son Paul, agreed to Jellinek's requests, and the Mercedes era was born. The name proved to be a great success, and soon all Daimler cars bore that name.

Karl Benz began Benz and Company in Mannheim, Germany, in 1883—a year after Gottlieb Daimler started his first company in Stuttgart. Like Daimler, Benz was a brilliant engineer and automobile enthusiast who demanded the highest quality. The two companies produced cars and made various advances in automobile technology as competitors for some thirty years until, in 1926, they joined to form the Daimler-Benz Company. They marketed their cars under the trade name Mercedes-Benz. In the judgment of many, the Mercedes-Benz was the finest car made anywhere.

over the years, and its incarnations decades later continue to have success today.

Gottlieb Daimler died of heart disease on March 6, 1900. Although he did not live to see the groundbreaking design for the Mercedes, Daimler's name became forever associated with the car that gained worldwide recognition for its extremely high quality. The Mercedes became so successful that the Daimler Motor Company in 1902 decided to use the name for all its cars, taking out a trademark for that purpose. The Daimler Company merged with its longtime competitor, the Benz Company, in 1926, and the Mercedes-Benz was established as arguably the finest car in the world.

Today, the Daimler-Chrysler family, which merged in 1998, continues to be a leader in successful car-making. Daimler's legacy continues in the vehicles and business that bear his name.

Timeline

1834
Gottlieb Wilhelm Daimler born in Schorndorf, Württemberg, Germany

1853–1857
Daimler works in a steam engine locomotive factory in Strasbourg

1863
Daimler meets Wilhelm Maybach

1872
Daimler becomes chief engineer at Deutz Gasmotoren-Fabrik

1882
Daimler and Maybach leave Deutz to set up a manufacturing plant

1883
Daimler invents and patents an ignition device

1885
Daimler and Maybach begin testing small engines on various vehicles

1890
Daimler founds Daimler Motoren-Gesellschaft

1900
Daimler dies; Maybach and Daimler's son develop the Mercedes

Inventor of the Diesel Engine

Rudolf Diesel

1858–1913

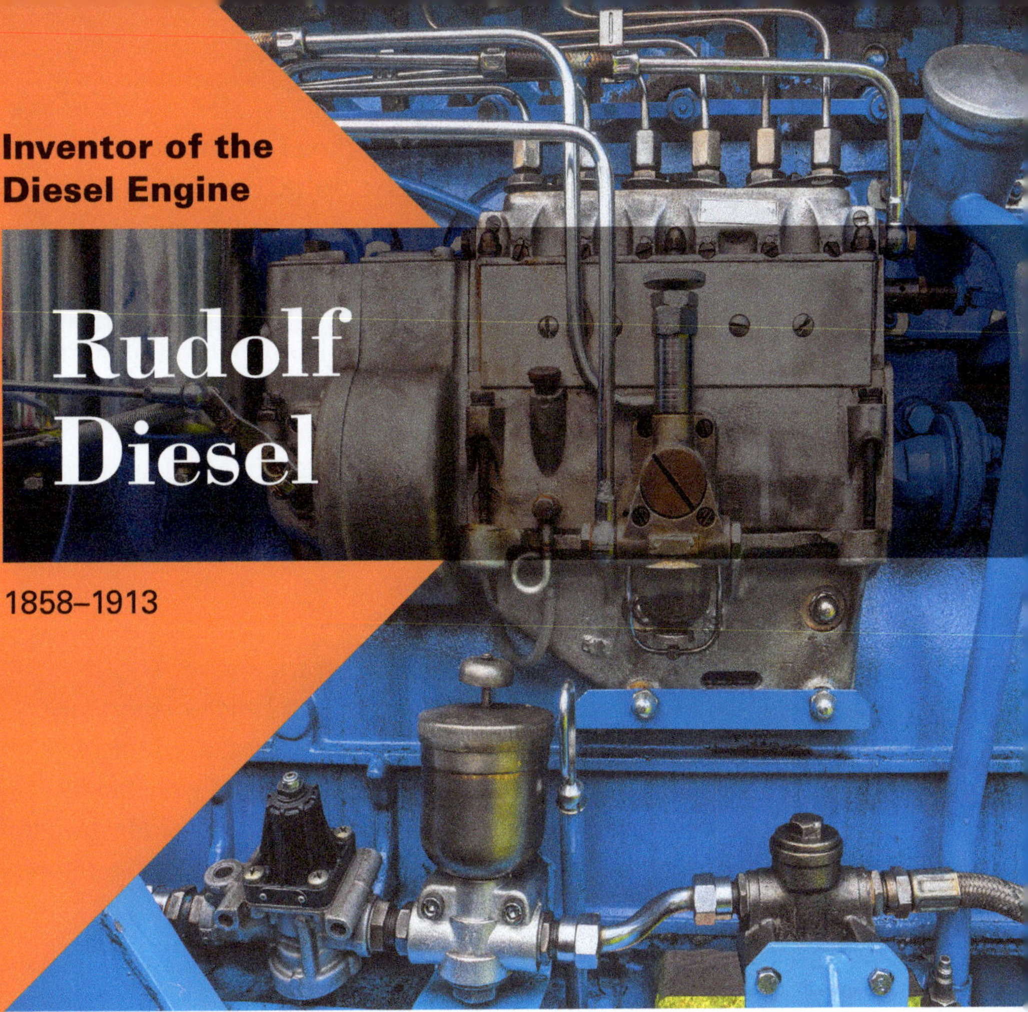

Not all inventors get to see their inventions come to fruition. Sometimes it is left to other inventors to take up the task of finishing the invention after the initial inventor has passed away. Such was the case with Rudolf Diesel and the type of fuel named after him. Today, diesel is a widely used fuel source that powers trucks, trains, ships, submarines, and power plants. What began as an idea resulted in the development of one of the most successful fuel sources in the world.

Beginnings

Rudolf Diesel's parents were German, and he lived much of his life in Germany, but he was born in Paris, France, on March 18, 1858,

Rudolf Diesel

and spent his childhood in that city. When Diesel was twelve, in 1870, war broke out between France and Germany, making it unsafe for Germans to remain in France. The family fled to England. Rudolf was soon sent to Germany, to his father's hometown, Augsburg, to continue his schooling. Later, he went to the Technische Hochschule (Technical High School) in Munich to study engineering.

There, Diesel became the pupil of Carl von Linde (1842–1934), a brilliant young German engineer who was in the process of inventing the technology used in modern refrigerators. By all accounts, Diesel was a dedicated student. In von Linde's laboratory, he learned about **thermodynamics** and heat engines, machines that extract the power locked in fuels such as coal and gasoline by alternately heating and cooling such fuels. In 1878, von Linde gave up his lecturing position to start a company manufacturing refrigerators. Two years later, Diesel joined him.

Defining the Problem

The nineteenth century was the heyday of the steam engine, which an Englishman, Thomas Newcomen (1664–1729), had invented around 1712. A steam engine is a type of heat engine that works like a giant kettle, burning coal to boil water and using the resulting steam to drive railroad locomotives and other machines. In a steam engine, the coal is burned to produce steam in one place (the boiler) and the steam makes useful power in another place (the cylinder, a large metal can with a piston that slides back and forth inside it). This process is called external combustion because the combustion (burning of the fuel) happens outside the cylinder. As the coal is burned, however, and the heat is transferred from the boiler to the cylinder, a great deal of energy is wasted, making steam engines very inefficient.

During the nineteenth century, a number of European inventors tried to develop engines that would use internal combustion. Instead of burning fuel outside the cylinder, the idea was to burn it inside the cylinder, a more efficient process that would waste less energy. The first person to suggest this, around 1800, seems to have been a French inventor named Philippe Lebon (1767–1804). Over the following decades, many other Europeans tried to make engines of this kind, with little success.

Finally, in 1876, German engineer Nikolaus Otto (1832–1891) made the first successful internal combustion engine. Otto's invention was a great improvement on the steam engine. It burned fuel and air inside a large metal cylinder in four separate stages or "strokes," known as the Otto cycle. In the first step, air and fuel entered the cylinder and mixed together. In the second step, a piston moved into the cylinder and compressed (squeezed) the mixture. This prepared for the third step: a spark of electricity set the mixture alight, causing a miniature explosion that pushed the piston back out of the cylinder, turned a crank, and generated power. In the fourth step, the piston pushed back into the cylinder to remove the exhaust gases produced by the burning fuel. This four-step cycle repeated itself, turning a constant supply of fuel into mechanical power. Otto's engine was ultimately reworked and revised into the gasoline engine that still powers most cars today.

"The automobile engine will come, and then I will consider my life's work complete."
—Rudolf Diesel

Designing the Solution

Diesel was unimpressed by Otto's engine. In his studies of thermodynamics, Diesel had learned that the best possible heat engine follows a series of steps called a Carnot cycle, named for its discoverer, French physicist Nicholas Sadi Carnot (1796–1832). Although Otto's engine was more efficient than a steam engine, it was less efficient than it might have been. Diesel believed he was a scientific genius and was certain he could make a better engine—and this was one reason he became an inventor.

The other reason was more ambitious. The Industrial Revolution, driven largely by the steam engine, had transformed society. Steam engines had made a small number of industrialists very wealthy and powerful, but ordinary people saw less benefit. Many struggled in dirty and unhealthy factories operating the machines; others worked long hours in underground mines digging the coal to power steam engines; and all benefited financially much less than their bosses. Rudolf Diesel realized that engines put power into the hands of ordinary people. He imagined a smaller, less expensive engine, running on affordable fuel, that would help artisans and small industrialists compete with the wealthy and powerful. Diesel's engine would be the people's engine.

Around 1890, Diesel figured out how to make his better internal combustion engine. Instead of using an electric spark, he burned the fuel-air mixture another way. When gases are compressed, they can heat up greatly—this is why a bicycle pump often gets hot during

Dreams of a Different Fuel

The gasoline and diesel burned in most vehicle engines comes from petroleum, a thick, brown liquid formed when plants and animals decay beneath rocks, either on land or offshore. Over millions of years, high temperatures and pressure turn the once-organic remains into a mixture of many different **hydrocarbons**. When these fossil fuels are burned in air, a chemical reaction called combustion takes place. This unlocks the energy stored in the fuel, producing heat that can power an engine. However, most materials will burn in air, so, theoretically, fuels other than petroleum could be used to drive engines.

Most diesel engines burn a low-grade and less expensive product of petroleum known as diesel, but that was never Rudolf Diesel's intention. One of his dreams was to create an engine that could run on almost any kind of fuel, even oil made from vegetables. He believed that this versatility would bring many benefits to society. It would free people from the need to buy expensive petroleum-derived fuel. Also, if communities grew crops to power their engines, farmers would benefit. Diesel's vision was that his engine could change society by putting more power into the hands of ordinary people and local communities.

use. Diesel used this effect to burn fuel in his engine. He built the engine around a long (10-foot; 3-meter) sturdy metal cylinder with a free-moving piston inside it. First, the cylinder filled with air. Then the piston compressed the air to about 1⁄20 of its original volume, making it extremely hot. Next, a pipe squirted droplets of fuel into the cylinder. Because the air and the cylinder were so hot, the fuel caught fire at once and gave off exhaust gas, which pushed the piston back out of the cylinder and turned a crank, much as in an Otto engine.

By 1892, Diesel had figured out the theory of his engine completely and was granted a patent. He published his ideas in 1893, and on August 10 of that year, his engine first ran successfully under its own power. The engine was still experimental, and Diesel spent several more years improving it. In December 1896, he demonstrated an engine that was about twice as efficient as a steam engine, getting twice as much power from the same amount of fuel by wasting less energy.

In the 1890s, the idea of making an engine that people could power with plant products seemed outrageous. Today, however, when demand for oil is high and people have greater concern for the environment, it seems less so. Unlike petroleum, which is a finite, or limited, resource, oils made from animal or vegetable fats are renewable: they could last forever. Many people are already exploring these alternative fuels. In the United States, many people drive dual-fuel cars, which can run on either alcohol derived from plants or traditional gasoline at the flick of a switch.

Elsewhere in the world, interest is growing in biodiesel, a fuel that can be made from many different organic materials, including soybeans, palm oil, peanut oil, hemp, animal and vegetable fats—and even the waste grease from cooking. Unlike petroleum, biodiesel has many environmental benefits. When it is produced from growing crops, it does not add to the problem of global warming. It is also nontoxic and produces fewer harmful emissions than traditional diesel or gasoline. Some states are actively promoting biodiesel. In Minnesota, for example, a state mandate has required all diesel fuel to contain at least 2 percent biodiesel since fall 2005.

Applying the Solution

From 1897 onward, Diesel promoted the invention tirelessly—so much so that he became ill from nervous exhaustion. His arrogance did not help. He claimed that few of the world's factories were good enough to build his engine and most should not even bother to try. In 1899, he set up his own plant in Augsburg to manufacture the device. He was no businessman, however, and work proceeded slowly because he had not ironed out all the problems associated with his engine's manufacture. Nevertheless, other engineers were impressed by what he had done and bought the rights to manufacture diesel engines to his design. This guaranteed he would soon become very wealthy.

Then tragedy struck. On September 29, 1913, while Diesel was traveling to London from Germany on the mail ship *Dresden*, he mysteriously vanished and was assumed to have fallen overboard. His body was found by another boat some days later, identified from papers in his pockets, and then buried at sea. Diesel's unusual death immediately aroused suspicion. Some people believe he committed suicide: he had always been a sensitive man, and the strain of working too hard may have caused him to take his life. Others have suggested he was murdered by either German or French agents who wanted to stop him from selling the secrets of the diesel engine to the British. However, it is equally likely that he simply fell overboard and drowned.

Honoring a Legend

Biodiesel enthusiasts honor Diesel as a visionary and a pioneer. Each August 10—the day Rudolf Diesel first successfully ran his engine—they celebrate International Biodiesel Day.

The Impact of the Solution on Society

The first commercial diesel engine was built not in Germany but in the United States. Adolphus Busch (1839–1913), the brewer of Budweiser beer, saw one of Diesel's models at an exhibition in Germany and realized how useful the invention would be. He bought the North

Today, along with large machines such as trains, many semitrucks run on diesel fuel.

American rights and built his own version, with Diesel's help, at his brewery in St. Louis, Missouri, in 1898. Working with Sulzer Brothers, a Swiss company, Busch developed an improved diesel engine and sold it throughout the United States and Canada. Busch-Sulzer engines were used in ships, ferries, factories, and power plants. During World War I (1914–1918), they powered many US submarines.

Diesel was convinced he had developed a brilliant invention, but his engine was not an immediate commercial success. Only after his death, when it became easier for engineers to experiment with his design, were smaller, more practical, and more successful diesel engines produced. In the United Kingdom, Dugald Clerk (1854–1932) simplified Diesel's four-stroke engine so that it worked using only two stages instead of four. That made the engine smaller and simpler. Two-stroke diesel engines were used in smaller power plants, water pumps, and ships. Shortly afterward, a compact "semi-diesel" engine was developed that combined the best features of the Otto and Diesel engines. It worked at lower pressures than a Diesel engine and used an electric spark to ignite the fuel, just like an Otto engine. The diesel-electric engine, which was a diesel engine connected to an electricity generator, was another modification. As this engine spun around, it turned the electricity generator and produced electricity to drive an electric motor at a much lower speed.

The first diesel engines were so large and heavy that they had to be fixed in place and could be used only in large factories and power plants. The efforts of many different engineers led to diesel engines gradually becoming small enough to be used in vehicles. They were used first to power large ships and railroad locomotives and later in smaller vehicles such as trucks and buses. The first diesel automobile was demonstrated in Germany in 1922, though diesel cars needed a sharp increase in gasoline prices, such as those of the 1970s, to become popular since they were a less-expensive option.

Today Diesel's inventions live on in history as revolutionary concepts that changed the way people perceived transportation. Many people were able to access vehicles after Diesel and Nikolaus Otto introduced their engines, making the population more powerful in their independence. Without revolutionary ideas from Diesel and others, society would be quite different and perhaps less autonomous than it is today.

Timeline

1858
Rudolf Diesel born in Paris, France

1890
Diesel devises his internal combustion engine

1892
Diesel receives a patent for his engine

1896
Diesel demonstrates an engine that is nearly twice as efficient as the steam engine

1899
Diesel establishes his own plant in Augsburg, Germany, to manufacture his engine

1913
Diesel dies mysteriously while en route to England

Inventor of the Model T and Moving Assembly Line

Henry Ford

1863–1947

Throughout the ages, perhaps no invention has been more transformative than the automobile. Henry Ford played a major role in developing the automobile's popularity among everyday Americans when he introduced the Model T car. Likewise, his concept of the assembly line revolutionized the way factories operated and gave more job opportunities to people who needed them. Over time, Ford and his car company have become staples of American entrepreneurialism. His legacy continues in the vehicles that bear his name.

Joining the World

Henry Ford's childhood was typical of a boy living in the United States in the mid-nineteenth century. He had been born in Greenfield, Michigan, on July 30, 1863, and he spent his days in a one-room schoolhouse and his evenings doing chores on the family farm. Machinery fascinated him; his mother called him a "born mechanic." At age twelve, he saw his first self-propelled vehicle, a giant coal-powered tractor, which seemed to him to be a messenger from the future. Ford would never forget the experience, later saying, "It was that engine which took me into automotive transportation."

Ford's family had been farmers for generations, and it was always assumed that he would take over the farm, but he had other ideas. At the age of sixteen, he walked to Detroit and arranged an apprenticeship with a mechanic. He also worked evenings in a watch-repair shop. He considered becoming a watch manufacturer until he realized that watches were a luxury, not a necessity. "Even then," he later remembered, "I wanted to make something in quantity."

For the next few years, Ford divided his time between engineering jobs and the farm. On the farm, he built a machine shop and a small, experimental "farm locomotive" to mechanize the chores he disliked so much. In 1884, his father promised him some timberland if he gave up being a mechanic. After meeting Clara Jane Bryant, he grudgingly agreed to his father's request so they could afford to wed. Ford married Clara in 1888 and their only son, Edsel, was born five years later.

Defining the Problem

Marriage brought responsibility, and it encouraged Ford to take a steadier job. In 1888, he became an engineer with the Detroit branch of the Edison Illuminating Company, the firm Thomas Edison (1847–1931) had established to bring electric light to the nation. Ford's job was to keep the power on, but he often had little to do. It was the perfect job for an inventor, and he spent the next five years trying to develop a practical gasoline-powered engine. After he succeeded, he was introduced to Thomas Edison at a company gathering; Edison praised Ford and encouraged him to "keep at it."

Designing the Solution

Having developed an engine, Ford next wanted to build an automobile. This he managed in 1896. The car he developed was not at all like modern cars. Named the Quadricycle, it ran on four 28-inch (71 cm) bicycle wheels with rubber tires and was steered by a large moving tiller at the front. When Ford tried out this "gasoline buggy" on the streets of Detroit, crowds gathered and terrified horses bolted in all directions.

Ford realized that if he could make one car, he could make many, but his hobby conflicted with his job at Edison. The company gave him a choice: it would promote him to general superintendent or he could go to work for himself. Confident, and with his wife's support, Ford chose the latter. In 1899, supported by a few wealthy backers, he formed the Detroit Automobile Company. For three years, Ford built luxury cars to order, but he wanted to make less expensive models that most people could afford.

In 1902, Ford decided to go his own way, and the following year he launched a new firm called the Ford Motor Company. By quitting his previous firm, he angered his investors, the very people who might have supported the new company. As a result, Ford had only $28,000 in

Henry Ford's Model T Touring Car on display

capital, most of it provided by ordinary citizens. In its first year of operation, the Ford Motor Company made a simple vehicle called the Model A, costing $850, and sold 1,708 of them. In 1908, after selling thousands of various models, Ford introduced his first truly affordable vehicle: the Model T. From then on, only one simple model would be offered and as Ford famously said, "Any customer can have a car painted any color that he wants so long as it is black." The customers loved it, and Ford sold cars by the million.

Applying the Solution

Ford's secret of success was mass production. His cars were gradually assembled by passing down a whole line of workers, a configuration known as an assembly line. The idea for the assembly line dates back to the nineteenth century. Eli Whitney (1765–1825) had developed a way of manufacturing rifles from standard pieces, a method that became known as mass production. Unlike the practice of a craft, in which one skilled worker makes one product from start to finish, mass production involves a group of workers, each making or handling only one piece of the product.

In 1913, Henry Ford took mass production to a new level by creating a conveyor belt pulled by a chain along the factory floor. The automated mechanism carried semi-completed car bodies past the line of workers who were putting them together. Each worker on the assembly line had a very specific job to do and an exact amount of time in which to do it if the whole system was to run smoothly.

Ford realized that automation was the key to manufacturing, but he also knew people were crucial to automation. Mass production was more tedious for workers than traditional craftwork. Assembly workers often did not stay on the job long, quitting to find more interesting work. Ford solved this problem in 1914 by introducing a $5-per-day minimum wage—twice what factory workers were typically earning at the time—and cutting the working day to just eight hours. This announcement made Ford's workers the best paid in the country, and it caused such a sensation that police had to be called to control crowds who massed outside the Ford factory to apply for work. Ford also built hospitals and schools for his workers and even introduced a profit-sharing plan. Critics worried that Ford was focusing too much on workers' welfare rather than profits: the *Wall Street Journal* suggested that actions like his were an "economic crime."

Ford could defy the critics because his firm was spectacularly successful. His attention to workers actually increased his success, and not only in car production. He never forgot the tedium and hard labor of farm work. Around the time he developed the Model T, he started tinkering with car parts to see if he could make what he called an "automobile plow," a combination of horse-drawn plow and automobile. The result of this effort was a tractor, the Fordson Model F, introduced in 1917, which did for agriculture what the Model T Ford did for driving. By using mass production methods, Ford cut the original price of the tractor from $750 to just $395. Eventually he sold 750,000 Fordson tractors and captured three-quarters of the US market.

Ford's Personal Life

With his company firmly established, Ford had time for other interests, including politics. He had strong opinions and never hesitated to express them. When World War I began in 1914, Ford, who was a pacifist, opposed the United States' involvement. In 1916, he rented a huge ocean liner, nicknamed the "Peace Ship," to sail to Europe in hopes of persuading the governments there to end the war—earning widespread ridicule. In 1918, he ran for the Senate in Michigan but was narrowly defeated.

Later, Ford's views prompted the *Chicago Tribune* to describe him as an "anarchist enemy of the nation" and an "ignorant idealist." In 1919, his attorney persuaded him to bring a $1 million libel suit against the newspaper. Three years earlier, Ford had quipped to a reporter from the *Tribune*, "History is more or less bunk." In the libel case, defense attorneys leaped on the remark with what one commentator described as "sadistic pleasure." They made Ford appear to be an ignorant fool by proving he could not answer the simplest questions about American history. Although he won the case, he was awarded not $1 million but six cents in damages. As he left the trial, he resolved to open a Henry Ford Museum "to show just what actually happened in years gone by."

Although Ford's views were controversial, they were generally conservative. He set up a "Sociological Department" at his factory to discourage his well-paid workers from wasting their money on things he disliked. If workers expected to earn their $5 per day, they had to have their homes inspected and prove they were sober and clean living. In other ways, Ford was extremely progressive. In the 1920s and 1930s, Ford's were among the only factories in the country to offer black workers equal opportunities.

In 1918, Ford had used his wealth to buy a newspaper, the *Dearborn Independent*, so he could promote his political views more easily. This got him into trouble when he started attacking Jews,

Changing Lives with the Model T

Henry Ford once vowed, "I will build a motor car for the great multitude, constructed of the best materials, by the best men to be hired, after the simplest designs that modern engineering can devise, so low in price that no man making a good salary will be unable to own one and enjoy with his family the blessing of hours of pleasure in God's great open spaces." When the Model T Ford went on sale in 1908, it achieved all these aims. Originally priced at $850, the touring model was well beyond the reach of most potential customers. However, Ford's innovative assembly line and his highly motivated workforce soon slashed the cost of making a Model T, and Ford passed the savings on to his customers. By 1913, he had cut the price to $600. Two years later it had dropped to $440, and by 1925 it was just $290, about a third of its original cost. At that price, even average families could buy a car—and with it they gained freedom. The Model T Ford even earned an affectionate nickname, the "Tin Lizzie," just like a member of the family.

Mass production brought other benefits. Since each worker was making only one piece of a car and all the pieces had to fit together, Ford had to use standardized components. Another of Ford's innovations had been to open dealerships where his cars could be sold; by 1912, he had seven thousand of these across the United States.

whom he claimed had been responsible for financing World War I. In 1920, his newspaper columns were published as a book called *The International Jew: The World's Foremost Problem*, which offended many people. He issued a public apology in 1927.

Ford's apparent anti-Semitism led some to suggest links with Adolf Hitler, the brutal dictator who led Germany from 1934 to 1945. Ford's writings against the Jews were widely read in Germany in the 1920s, and some historians have speculated that they may have aided Hitler's rise to power. It is known that Hitler greatly admired Ford and kept a photograph of him on his wall. He even awarded Ford a medal for building a factory in Berlin to make trucks and tanks for the German military.

Mass production made repairs easier for dealers because they could use standardized spares. The process of putting a car together also had to be simple so cars could be assembled as quickly as possible. In 1912, it took the Ford workers about half a day (twelve hours) to build each vehicle; two years later, they could make a car in ninety minutes. Customers also benefited because they could make basic repairs, such as changing tires, themselves.

The Model T's brilliance is difficult to appreciate in the twenty-first century. It is almost inconceivable today that a company could offer for sale a car that remained almost unchanged for twenty years and still sell fifteen million. Between 1908 and 1927, more than half the cars sold in the United Sates were Model T Fords. When Henry Ford constructed his giant River Rouge plant in the 1920s, he did not have to borrow so much as a cent to do it. All the money he needed for this ambitious plan came from profits earned by the Model T.

Ford's idea of an affordable car was gradually copied by other manufacturers. The German carmaker Volkswagen even took its name from the idea; *Volkswagen* is German for "people's car." Basic, functional, and highly affordable, the car remains just as popular in the modern world as it was in Ford's own time a century ago.

Although his cars and tractors were changing the face of America, Ford was nostalgic for an earlier and simpler time. He financed a radio show in which rural stories were read on air to his workers. In 1933, he expanded his museum into a historical theme park and school named Greenfield Village. Built in the style of a rural town, it incorporated reproductions of one hundred buildings of major historical significance and has been a popular educational and tourist attraction ever since. Ford wanted to preserve the past but not live in it. As he wrote in his autobiography, "What is past is useful only as it suggests ways and means for progress."

As he grew older, Ford became more set in his ways. Although his son, Edsel, became the nominal president of his company in 1919, Henry Ford still made all the key decisions, frequently overturning those made by Edsel. Ford's extraordinary success made him reluctant to change, but the world was evolving. Even when the General Motors Company began to challenge Ford's market share, Ford continued to make only one car, the Model T, never altering it from one year to the next. Ford's view was simple: "There is a tendency to keep monkeying with styles and to spoil a good thing by changing it." Toward the end of the 1920s, however, after Ford had sold more than fifteen million Model Ts, he introduced a different car—named Model A, like the first vehicle he produced in 1903—to replace it. In the 1930s, he finally joined the rest of the car-making business and introduced a new model each year.

Not only car manufacturing had moved on, though. Workers' expectations had also changed. By the 1930s, Ford was paying less than the industry average, and his workers were demanding to join unions. Ford resisted, turning his Sociological Department into a bullying police force called the Service Department. Run by a former boxer, it started cracking down on union organizers. In 1937, when the Service Department clashed with union officials at Ford's giant River Rouge plant, a small riot followed and sixteen people were injured. After a major legal action and a strike at River Rouge, Ford was forced to choose between shutting down the factory and allowing in the unions. Grudgingly, he relented.

Continuing the Legacy

When Edsel Ford died of cancer in 1943, at only forty-nine years of age, the presidency of the Ford Motor Company reverted to his deeply saddened father. As the company's fortunes continued to decline, however, people questioned whether Henry Ford was the best person to run the company he had founded. The stubbornness and determination that had made him one of the greatest industrialists of all time now took his company to the brink of ruin. During the late 1930s, the company had been losing an estimated $1 million every

Ford's Car Plant

The enormous car plant Henry Ford created at River Rouge, Michigan, in the 1920s was a testament to his towering ambition. With eighty-one thousand on the payroll and a total floor space of nearly seven million square feet, the plant—not surprisingly—cost almost $270 million. This was a phenomenal sum early in the twentieth century and prompted outrage among Ford's original shareholders: they feared such a massive investment would seriously dent the company's profits. Henry Ford had to buy out their shares personally so he could continue with his expensive plan.

Ford's idea was to build the world's largest car plant so he could cut the price of the Model T still further. His philosophy of car manufacturing was: "Reduce the price, extend the operations, and improve the article." However, he soon realized he would also need to lower the cost of raw materials. That prompted moves to make River Rouge entirely self-sufficient. Thus, the plant burned coal from Ford's own mines in Kentucky, and it used steel manufactured from his iron mines in Michigan, wood from his forests in Minnesota, rubber from the company's plantations in Brazil, and windows made in River Rouge's own glassworks. Although it was a logical idea for making cars less expensively, maintaining huge plants like River Rouge meant the company could not respond as quickly to consumer demand, a problem that hastened the Ford Motor Company's decline in the 1930s.

day. World War II brought a respite. Although Ford again opposed the United States' involvement, he saw no contradiction in helping the government to manufacture thousands of warplanes at a huge new plant built specifically for the purpose.

When the war ended in 1945, Ford's reign ended, too. Control passed to his grandson, Henry Ford II, and Henry Ford the founder receded into the background. He died two years later, on April 7, 1947, in Dearborn, leaving a personal estate estimated at nearly $1 billion.

The Impact of the Solution on Society

Only twenty-eight when he took charge, Henry Ford II rapidly restored the Ford Motor Company's fortunes. He brought in new managers, modernized the business, and turned it into a global organization with bases in more than thirty countries. Although his grandfather had insisted on keeping control of the company in the family and private, Henry Ford II took Ford Motor public in 1956. This stock offering, which raised $650 million, was the largest stock offering in the United States at that time. Two years later, the company launched a radical new model, named the Edsel as a tribute to the late Edsel Ford. Despite being technically innovative and heavily advertised, the Edsel was a flop and the company was forced

The Ford Motor Company continues to have much success selling cars in the United States and around the world.

to scrap it within three years. This episode cost the company almost half the money it had made through the stock offering. Ford quickly recovered, however, remaining one of the world's largest industrial corporations into the twenty-first century.

Despite Henry Ford's eventual departure from the company, his business and the cars for which we would become known had a tremendous impact on society. Before his introduction of the Model T and the assembly line, many people lived outside cities, dependent on farms to make a living. By the time he had left the company, more people had moved into the cities and were making a living working in factories. There is no doubt Henry Ford contributed to the industrial revolution ignited in the United States. His products and company continue to have a place in modern-day society, and his name will always have a place in history books.

Timeline

1863
Henry Ford born in Greenfield, Michigan

1869
Ford begins an apprenticeship as a mechanic

1888
Ford works as an engineer in Detroit

1896
Ford builds his first automobile

1899
Ford forms the Detroit Automobile Company

1902
Ford starts the Ford Motor Company

1908
Ford launches the Model T

1917
Ford launches the Fordson Model F tractor

1945
Ford retires from Ford Motor Company

1947
Ford dies

Inventor of the Global Positioning System

Ivan A. Getting

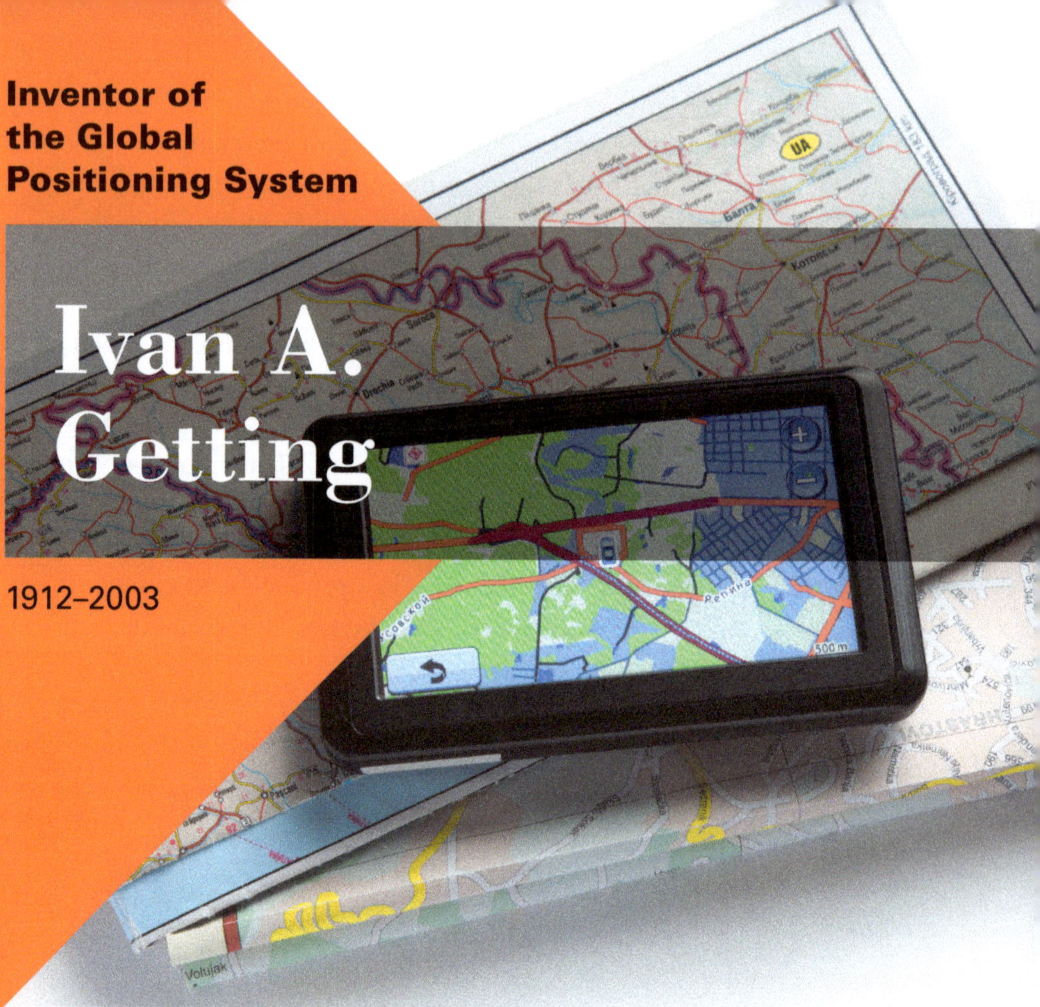

1912–2003

When you want to go on a road trip, oftentimes you will bring a navigational device called a Global Positioning System (GPS). Sometimes this is an app on your phone or a system in your car. It is an electronic mapping device that guides you to where you want to go. However, its origins began in the military, with inventor Ivan Getting as its creator. Since its introduction to the public, the GPS has transformed the way people move around the globe.

An Inventor Begins

Ivan Alexander Getting was born in New York City in 1912. His family was originally from what is now Slovakia. Getting grew up mainly in Pittsburgh, Pennsylvania, but he spent the year 1919 living and attending school in Bratislava, in what was then Czechoslovakia.

Getting won a scholarship to the Massachusetts Institute of Technology (MIT) in Cambridge, Massachusetts. Graduating in 1933 in the midst of the Great Depression, he was unable to find a job, so he applied for a Rhodes scholarship to Oxford University in England. He was awarded a scholarship and earned his doctorate in astrophysics from Oxford in 1935.

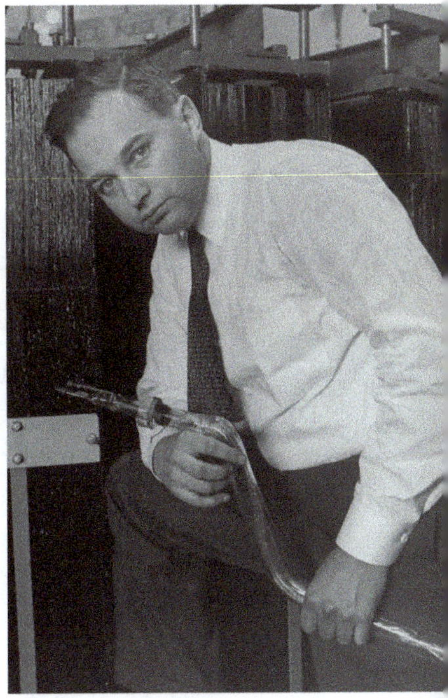

Ivan Getting working in his laboratory at MIT

Getting then decided to return to the United States, accepting an offer to become a junior fellow at Harvard University in Cambridge, Massachusetts. While working there on a problem involving cosmic rays, Getting developed a type of circuit called a flip-flop, so named because it can go back and forth between two states, to help him with his work. His circuit was much faster than any other flip-flop then in use, and as computers developed, Getting's circuit would end up being widely employed to create what is known as **temporary memory**.

Getting, however, was moving on to yet another field: nuclear physics. His reasons for choosing this field were rooted in the real world. In 1939, physicists in Nazi Germany split the atom, paving the way for the development of the atomic bomb. By 1940, Nazi Germany had conquered almost all of western Europe.

Although the United States would not formally enter World War II until December 1941, by 1940 the US government, convinced that conflict with Germany was inevitable, undertook a major push into weapons research in conjunction with various universities. Getting was approached in the fall of 1940 by an acquaintance, who asked if he wanted to join a new laboratory at MIT that was going to create new forms of defense technology. Getting jumped at the chance—even though he was unsure exactly what work at the lab would involve.

Getting joined the Radiation Laboratory, or RadLab, at MIT. The RadLab focused on developing and improving radar (radio detection and ranging), which was poorly understood at the time. Radar uses radio waves to calculate the position of objects. Getting directed the laboratory's army radar division and contributed to many of the RadLab's projects, most notably the development of a radar system to target the German V-1 and V-2 flying bombs.

The V-1 (Vergeltungswaffe 1, or "retaliation weapon 1") and V-2 were guided, unmanned bombs. As the bombs were small and very fast, conventional antiaircraft fire was almost useless against them. Beginning in mid-1944, Nazi Germany hammered Great Britain, in particular London, with V-1 and V-2 attacks. Getting helped develop

Working GPS

Getting developed GPS because his experiences in World War II had taught him the importance of location. "Position in the military sense is very essential," he said. "Knowing exactly where you are is extremely important. Knowing exactly where the enemy is [is] important."

GPS has two major components: satellites in space and receivers on Earth. Communication between the satellites and the receiver informs a user of his or her position. Each GPS satellite is locked into a precise orbit around Earth so that at any given time four satellites are in reach of a receiver from any point on Earth. The satellites emit radio signals to the receivers, which are programmed with a guide telling them where each of the satellites is in space.

To determine a user's location, the receiver calculates the time taken for a signal to arrive from the four satellites. The signals are sent simultaneously, but a signal emitted by a satellite located farther away from a receiver will take longer to reach it. Such brief lags in the signal are enough for the receiver to calculate its distance from each of the four satellites. Once the receiver knows the satellites' locations in space, and its distance from the satellites, it is able to determine its own position on Earth.

a radar tracking system that would detect and automatically follow a target. Such aiming systems proved devastatingly effective against V-1 and V-2 bombs.

In 1945, Nazi Germany was defeated and World War II came to an end. Getting remained at MIT as a professor of electrical engineering until 1950, when the outbreak of the Korean War made him decide to focus again on defense work.

Getting worked for the US Air Force until 1951, when he joined the defense contractor Raytheon as vice president for research and engineering, a position he held until 1960. At Raytheon, Getting helped develop the Sparrow III and Hawk radar-guided missile systems, which are still in use.

In 1960, Getting resigned from Raytheon to become the founding president of the Aerospace Corporation, a nonprofit research organization in El Segundo, California, established to help the US Air Force with its space programs. Aerospace made many contributions to the space program, including helping to develop the Mercury and Gemini missions.

In the late 1960s, Aerospace was slated to help create a manned space station for the air force. Getting geared up his company for the effort, hiring hundreds of new people. Then, in 1969, the station was suddenly canceled, leaving Aerospace's new staff with nothing to do.

A committee had been established to decide on the direction of the US space program. Getting suggested several projects to the committee in hopes that the projects would lead to new work for Aerospace, thus preventing layoffs. Among his suggestions was a new system of navigation, the Global Positioning System (GPS).

Defining the Problem

Getting would later say that the idea of GPS emerged from his experiences during World War II, which made him realize the importance of knowing exact locations in combat. Ground-based navigation systems can be blocked by natural formations such as mountains and hampered by bad weather; in addition, the curvature of the earth limits their range.

Space satellites opened up the possibility of a new global navigation system. The US Department of Defense had decided that all the military branches should be on a single navigational system, and a global, weatherproof system like GPS seemed ideal.

Designing the Solution

Day-to-day development and management of GPS during the 1970s was the responsibility of Colonel Bradford Parkinson of the air force. Getting remained involved nonetheless. By this point in his career, Getting was enormously respected within the military community for his many contributions to defense technology, and he used his stature to ensure that the very expensive GPS project was kept on track and not allowed to languish.

In 1978, a year after Getting retired from Aerospace, the first experimental GPS satellite was launched; nine more satellites were launched during the 1980s. In 1989, the first satellite for the current GPS was launched, and by 1994 the last of the twenty-four satellites was launched, creating what is the Navstar satellite system.

Applying the Solution

Although GPS was a US Department of Defense project, from the beginning it was clear that the system could be very useful for civilians in need of navigational guidance—for example, backpackers or boaters. Making GPS available to civilians could have created a security threat, however, if a hostile army outfitted its troops with GPS receivers. The Navstar system was designed to emit two signals: one to be received by ordinary GPS receivers and one to be received only by the US military's receivers. The military signal was made more accurate, to allow a military receiver to indicate a user's position within 30 to 60 feet (9 to 18 m).

The civilian signal was made less accurate and reported a user's position within 90 feet (27 m). However, military planners worried that the difference in accuracy between the two systems was not great enough to give military signal users the advantage. When the GPS system first became operational in 1993, the civilian signal was degraded further to restrict a civilian GPS receiver to reporting positions within 300 feet (91 m).

As the 1990s progressed, pilots of boats and airplanes began to rely more and more on GPS receivers. The US government became concerned that the degraded civilian signal could lead to serious boat and airplane accidents. As GPS receivers became increasingly popular, these worries began to outweigh military concerns. In 2000, the US government restored the accuracy of the civilian GPS signal. If necessary, the signal can again be degraded.

The Impact of the Solution on Society

The increased accuracy of civilian GPS, combined with smaller, cheaper receivers, increased the system's popularity with the public. Among the many civilian GPS users was Getting, who in February 2003 shared the Draper Prize, a prestigious engineering award, with Parkinson for their joint work on GPS. Eight months later, Getting died at his home in Coronado, California, at the age of ninety-one.

Modern GPS systems like this one are included in many cars and other modes of transportation.

In the twenty-first century, civilian GPS receivers have much success. Many cars and phones now have GPS integrated into them. However, one suggested downfall of GPS is that people have become reliant on it to go on trips across a country, or even within the city in which they live. Rather than using their initiative and printed maps, they depend on GPS. Nevertheless, Getting's invention has influenced society in many ways and will continue to do so for years to come.

Timeline

1912
Ivan Getting born in New York City

1935
Getting earns a doctorate in astrophysics from Oxford University

1940
Getting joins the Radiation Laboratory (RadLab) at MIT

1945
Getting works as a professor of electrical engineering at MIT

1960
Getting founds the Aerospace Corporation

1969
Getting begins to develop the Global Positioning System (GPS)

1977
Getting retires from Aerospace

1978
The first experimental GPS satellite is launched

1994
The Navstar satellite system is completed

2003
Getting wins the Draper Prize; he dies later that year

Developer of the Bicycle

Pierre Michaux

1813–1883

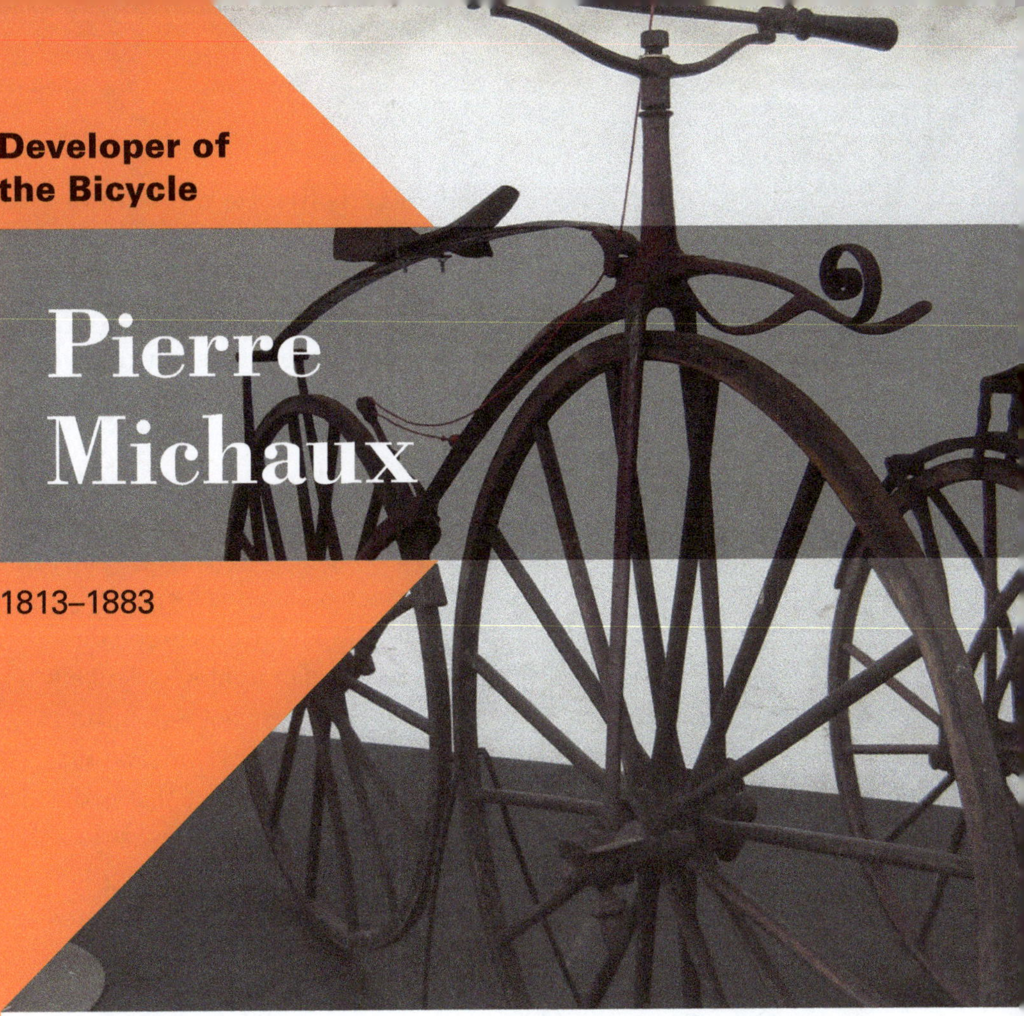

In all sorts of weather you can see people on streets riding bicycles. These vehicles of transportation have been enjoyed by many people for over two hundred years and continue to be a reliable mode of transport today. However, the modern bicycle was not invented by one person at one specific time. Rather, it was the contribution of many people's ideas that culminated in the creation of the bicycle we know today. One of the most influential inventors of the bicycle was Pierre Michaux, who is often credited with being the modern-day bicycle's inventor.

Growing Up

Little is known about Pierre Michaux's early life. He was born in Bar-le-Duc, in northeast France, in 1813. At some point, Michaux moved to Paris.

By the mid-1860s, Michaux had a blacksmith's shop in Paris, and he had four sons. At least one of them, Ernest, would work with Pierre in his shop.

Pierre Michaux's son, Ernest Michaux, poses with a Michaux velocipede in this portrait.

Defining the Problem

In 1867, Michaux's shop began running advertisements for a device called a velocipede. To contemporary observers, the velocipede might have looked odd but it was not unfamiliar; it was an improvement on the draisine, a machine that had had a brief period of popularity in the late 1810s.

The draisine was patented in 1818 by a German baron, Karl von Drais, a forester who had wanted to make his long walks through the forest easier and faster. The draisine had two wheels and was pushed along by the feet. It was popular for a very short time; the fad petered out in the early 1820s.

Over the next few decades, other inventors tried to produce new vehicles that, like the draisine, could be powered by a human rider—a category of vehicles that became known as velocipedes. The vast majority of these had three or four wheels, not two. Inventors of the day believed that a two-wheeled vehicle would work only if the rider's feet touched the ground. Otherwise, the vehicle would surely tip over.

Designing the Solution

The Michaux velocipede, therefore, was a conceptual breakthrough when it was introduced in the 1860s. It was built like a draisine, with two wheels, one in front of the other, but it had a foot crank attached directly to the front wheel, as on a modern tricycle. Instead of keeping their feet on the ground as with a draisine, riders would use their feet to pedal the vehicle along. New riders were pleasantly surprised to discover that balancing on the vehicle was relatively easy, especially once the bicycle was in motion. This concept of balancing on two wheels is what led historians to consider the Michaux velocipede the first true bicycle.

Applying the Solution

Like the draisine, the bicycle was expensive—costing almost as much as a horse-drawn carriage. It looked, if anything, even stranger than a draisine. Nonetheless, by 1870, thousands of bicycles were being sold, dozens of other manufacturers had entered the bicycle business, and the first cycling magazine was being published.

One reason for this popularity was the ingenuity of Michaux's marketing, which helped to create interest in the new device. Since most people were skeptical about their ability to ride a bicycle, lessons were included in the price of purchase. Michaux bicycles were ubiquitous at the International Exhibition, a huge fair held in Paris in 1867. The company sponsored bicycle races that drew thousands of spectators. Michaux's company even added a steam engine to one of its bicycles, creating the first motorcycle, which was capable of speeds of almost 20 miles per hour (32 kmh).

In 1869, Michaux had accepted a buyout offer from three brothers of the wealthy Olivier family. Under the agreement, Michaux was forbidden to market bicycles or other velocipedes under his own name. He ignored these stipulations and began selling his own Michaux-brand bicycles, so the Oliviers took him to court.

During the trial, the Olivier brothers made an extraordinary claim. René Olivier testified that he and his brothers had become fascinated by the idea of a bicycle in the mid-1860s. They needed someone with the technical expertise to actually build one, so they had selected Michaux and provided him with the design. Their father was a prominent industrialist in Lyon who was not happy about his sons' latest interest, so they used the name Michaux on the bicycles instead of their own.

"Let me tell you what I think of bicycling. I think it has done more to emancipate women than anything else in the world. I stand and rejoice every time I see a woman ride by on a wheel."
—Susan B. Anthony

According to the Oliviers, René Olivier actually ran Michaux's business, and Michaux himself was little more than a figurehead. In addition, René Olivier maintained, it had not been Michaux's idea to add a foot pedal to a draisine. He claimed it was the idea of an unnamed workman.

The court found that Michaux had violated the severance agreement. The Oliviers' victory in court did not ensure the continued success of their bicycle business, however; the next year, France went to war with Prussia (now part of Germany). The war was a disaster for France, and the market for bicycles collapsed in the resulting turmoil. The damages Michaux had to pay the Oliviers and the overall collapse of the French bicycle market bankrupted him, and Michaux died in a pauper's hospice in Paris in 1883.

After a man named Pierre Lallement failed to bring the concept of the bicycle to the United States, the development of the bicycle would continue in a country where the roads were relatively well paved, where no one owned an overarching patent, and where no devastating war was in progress—Great Britain. Like the Americans, the British were first introduced to Michaux bicycles when they were imported into the country. The bicycles were promptly nicknamed "boneshakers" for the uncomfortable ride delivered by their hard tires.

Despite the discomfort, bicycles began to catch on with the British public. One reason was the introduction of the high-rise bicycle in the late 1860s. Because the foot pedals were connected directly to the front wheel, the larger the wheel, the faster the bicycle would travel with the same amount of human effort. The result was bicycles with front wheels that were 5 or 6 feet (1.5 or 1.8 m) in diameter, limited only by the length of a rider's legs. The rider sat directly over the wheel, at the highest point of the bicycle. This design had a serious flaw: collisions could result in potentially fatal falls.

In the mid-1880s, British bicycle manufacturers developed a safer design. Instead of connecting pedals directly to the front wheel, they connected the pedals to a gear and then used a chain to connect that gear to the back wheel. As a result, when a rider pedaled, the back

Bicycle Before Michaux

The draisine invented by Karl von Drais looks quite similar to a modern bicycle. Indeed, historians disagree as to whether the draisine should be considered a bicycle. The draisine had two wheels, one behind the other, which were linked by a piece of wood that also supported a seat. As with a bicycle, the front wheel could be steered with handles. What separates the draisine from the bicycle in the minds of many historians is the lack of pedals. Von Drais's idea was to make a machine that would make walking faster and less tiring. Instead of pedaling the machine along, the draisine rider pushed with his feet against the ground as though he were taking a walk.

The draisine caught on briefly in continental Europe and in Great Britain, where it was also called a hobbyhorse. It was an expensive device, and many considered it flamboyant: the English also called it a dandyhorse, since only "dandies"—wealthy and fashionable young men—seemed to ride it. Traveling by draisine could be faster than traveling on foot; von Drais claimed that he could reach a speed of 12 miles per hour (19 kmh), which was as fast as traveling on horseback. Draisines required smooth roads, however. Such roads were quite rare at the time, limiting the draisine's usefulness.

wheel turned, resulting in the same effect of directly pedaling a much larger wheel. These bicycles, called safety bikes, were tremendously successful, in no small part because unlike a high-rise, they could be ridden by someone wearing a skirt—almost all women wore skirts in those days. By the late 1880s, an estimated half a million bicycles and tricycles were in use in Great Britain.

Another innovation in the 1880s would make the bicycle even more popular. In 1888, Scots veterinarian John Dunlop, trying to improve his son's tricycle, conceived the idea of using inflatable

Mystery Man

Pierre Lallement, ca. 1870

Even assuming that René Olivier told the truth in his testimony about the origins of the bicycle, the mystery of the unnamed workman remained. Historians have suggested that the mystery workman, Pierre Lallement, was the only person to have patented a Michaux-style bicycle.

Lallement, who was French, patented the bicycle in the United States in 1866. Later in life, he would say that he had conceived the idea for the bicycle in 1862 while working as a machinist in Nancy, in eastern France. He saw a man go by on a draisine and was so impressed by the unusual machine that he began to develop one of his own. He moved to Paris to work in a velocipede shop, and he perfected his bicycle in the summer of 1863, riding it around the streets for all to see.

As with the Oliviers, it is impossible to know for certain whether Lallement was telling the truth, since he gave his account many years rubber tires rather than solid tires. The pneumatic tire resulted in a ride that was not only far more comfortable, but faster, making the bicycle a truly practical means of transportation.

The Impact of the Solution on Society

The pneumatic tire would eventually prove important to the development of another form of transportation now popular: the automobile. As the improved bicycle caught on in the United States and continental Europe, bicyclists demanded better roads, which the automobile would later exploit.

after the bicycle was invented. Some historians have suggested that Lallement discovered Michaux's design in France and then claimed it as his own in the United States. It is also possible, as René Olivier's testimony implies, that Michaux obtained Lallement's design.

Records show, however, that Lallement moved to the United States, received his patent in 1866, and tried to go into the bicycle business in Connecticut. The venture was not immediately successful; by 1868, Lallement had returned to France and opened his own bicycle business there. That year the bicycle became popular in the United States because Michaux bicycles were brought from France and were copied by American manufacturers.

Lallement inadvertently helped to stifle the bicycle industry in the United States, however, by selling his patent to Calvin Witty. In 1869, Witty sent a letter to every bicycle manufacturer in the United States, demanding large fees for use of the patent.

In addition to the patent issue, American bicycle manufacturers faced another problem: like the draisine, early bicycles required smooth roads to work properly, and most roads in the United States were not nearly smooth enough. Cyclists took to the sidewalks instead, creating a hazard to pedestrians. Towns began to ban bicycles, and, as in France, the bicycle fad in the United States quickly fizzled out.

Today bicycles continue to have importance in society. Many people around the world use them daily to get around their cities or villages. The bicycle is a significant vehicle that has inspired others to create similar devices. Each year new models of bicycles are produced. Some people use them as a form of exercise, while others use them to navigate their hometowns or to commute to work. Regardless who invented it, the bicycle is an influential invention that will continue to impact society for many years.

Timeline

1813
Pierre Michaux born in Bar-le-Duc, France

1867
Michaux has a blacksmith shop in Paris

Mid-1860s
Michaux's shop runs advertisements for a velocipede

1869
Michaux is bought out by the Olivier family

1883
Michaux dies

Inventors of the Hot Air Balloon

Joseph-Michel Montgolfier and Jacques-Étienne Montgolfier

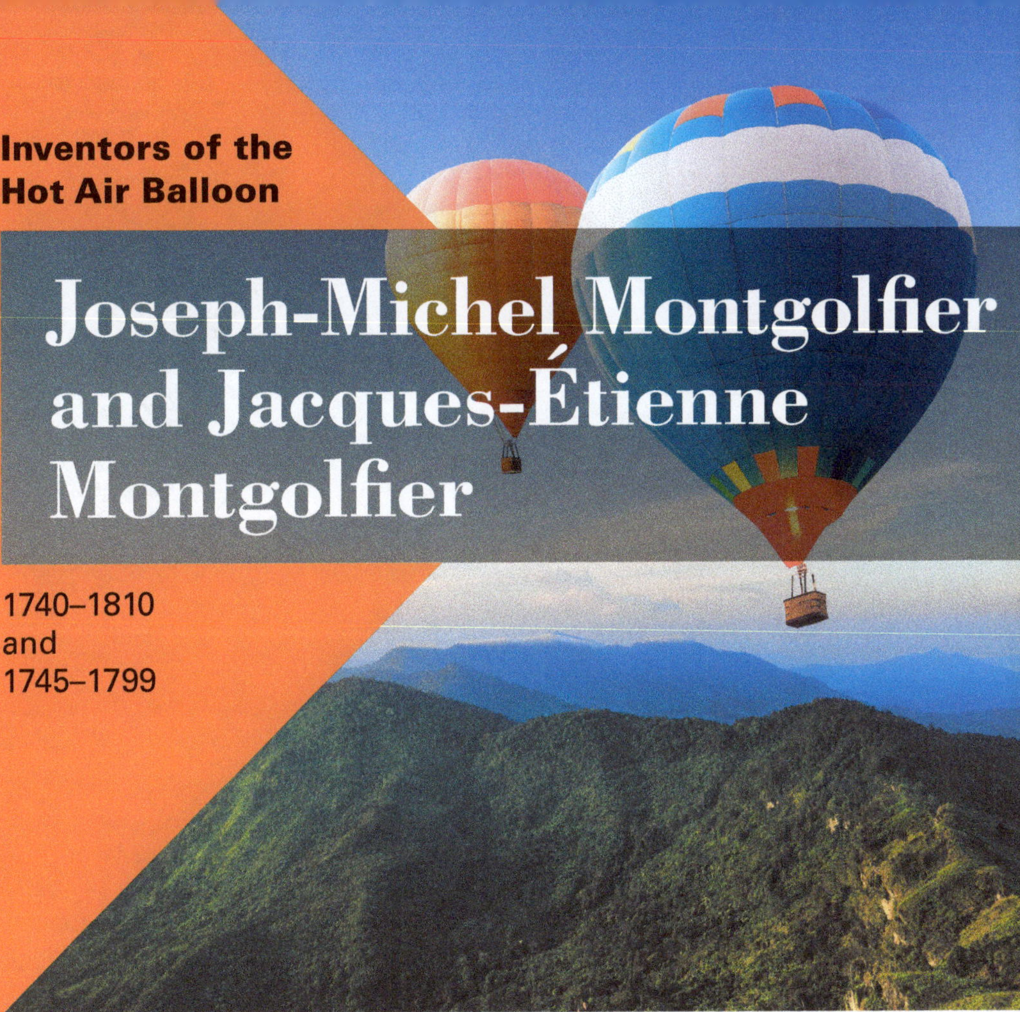

1740–1810
and
1745–1799

People have tried many different methods of air travel since early concepts were first envisioned. From fashioning their own wings to creating hovercrafts, airplanes, and helicopters, the world has been inspired to travel through the air in remarkable creations. In the 1700s, two brothers created the first hot air balloon. Today, hot air balloons are popular for tourists and people who want to experience a unique form of air transport. While it is not a main means of transport today, the hot air balloon exists as a present link to the past.

Portraits of Joseph-Michel Montgolfier (*left*) and Jacques-Étienne Montgolfier (*right*)

Brother Inventors

Joseph-Michel Montgolfier and Jacques-Étienne Montgolfier (who went by his middle name) were two of the sixteen children of Pierre Montgolfier, a papermaker living in the small town of Vidalon in southern France. The papermaking business was large, with various family members running a number of different mills in the region. Pierre Montgolfier oversaw the entire operation, and he groomed his eldest son, Raymond, to be his successor.

Joseph, who was born in 1740, was never a candidate for that responsibility. Although Joseph was bright, especially in mathematics and science, he was thought to be absentminded and undisciplined. Despite his father's best efforts to obtain a good education for his son, Joseph failed once in school and ran away twice. The second time Joseph ran away from school, he was in his late teens and could not be coaxed back.

In contrast, Étienne, who was born in 1745, was a very responsible and diligent student who was eventually sent to Paris to study architecture. While in Paris, Étienne worked for a number of businessmen, including Jean-Baptiste Réveillon, a successful manufacturer of wallpaper.

Étienne did so well in Paris that in 1772, when his brother Raymond died unexpectedly, he was instructed to take over the family business despite being the youngest of the family's four surviving sons. Étienne returned to Vidalon that same year and took leadership of his family's affairs at the age of twenty-seven. Joseph and Étienne continued to work in the family business for the next several years.

Defining the Problem

In November 1782, Joseph, who was now living in Avignon, was sitting in his house one evening. According to his later recollection, he was looking at a print depicting a siege of a fortress on the island of Gibraltar, which had been under attack for three years. Because it was on an island, the fortress could easily repel attacks by land or by sea, and it occurred to Joseph that Gibraltar might be attacked from above if a way could be devised to get troops up into the air. He looked over at his fireplace, where a fire was burning. Some force, he realized, was driving cinders and ash up the chimney. Might not that same force be used to drive other things up into the air as well?

Joseph set up an experiment to test his idea. He built a lightweight box out of taffeta and thin strips of wood with an opening at the bottom. He then set it on a stand over a small fire. It floated off the stand and all the way up to the ceiling.

Designing the Solution

Excited, Joseph returned to the family home in Vidalon and enlisted Étienne's help to develop his idea. Throughout December 1782, the two built ever-bigger taffeta boxes, which rose with such force when put over a fire that one broke the cords holding it down and floated more than a mile before landing.

Étienne began improving on Joseph's original idea, making the switch from a box shape to a bag-shaped balloon, which rose more easily and had more lift. Taffeta balloons seemed to lose lift quickly, so the brothers switched to paper backed with fabric.

Their experimental balloons kept escaping, occasionally frightening the neighbors. The Montgolfiers became worried that someone else would eventually realize what they were doing, copy their work, and take credit for the invention. To prevent this, on June 4, 1783, the Montgolfiers held a public demonstration of the hot air balloon in Annonay, a city near Vidalon. The balloon, which was 35 feet (11 m) wide, was unmanned. Under the balloon itself was an iron basket filled with shredded wool and dry straw, which was set on fire. The balloon inflated, rose 3,000 feet (914 m) into the air, and floated for a mile and a half before landing. The demonstration was the subject of countless newspaper stories all across France. Both the size of the balloon and the height it attained suggested to observers that it might be used to carry a person into the air.

Applying the Solution

Both brothers were hoping that the French government could be persuaded to fund further balloon construction and experimentation, in part because their father did not want any more family money spent

The First Experiment

Joseph's first experiment using a fire to launch a small taffeta box into the air might not seem exciting today. However, at the time it was a major conceptual leap because no one had harnessed this kind of lifting force before.

The idea of harnessing lift was a novel one. When hydrogen was identified in 1766, it was common knowledge among scientists that hydrogen was much lighter than air. Yet no one tried to make a large hydrogen balloon until news of the Montgolfiers' accomplishments spread across France.

Joseph could not explain why the fire had lifted up the box. He speculated that the lifting action might be due to the presence of smoke or that some sort of chemical reaction might be taking place that made the "rarefied air" coming out of a flame lighter than the regular air. It was not until late 1783 that scientists agreed on what was actually lifting the Montgolfier balloon: hot air, they discovered, was less dense than cool air, so it would rise.

on their invention. Since Étienne was the more practical and sociable of the two, he traveled to Paris in the summer of 1783 to lobby officials for funding.

Étienne also had an important connection in Paris: Réveillon, the wallpaper manufacturer. The two men were friends, and Réveillon helped to improve the design and construction of the hot air balloon. He suggested that instead of using paper and cloth, which would fall apart in the rain, the balloon should be made of cloth that had been sealed with varnish. In addition, Réveillon insisted that the Montgolfier balloons be ornately decorated with colorful printed designs.

Étienne was able to obtain permission to conduct a ballooning exhibit for King Louis XVI at the royal palace in Versailles in September 1783. At the time, concerns were voiced that living creatures would not be able to survive a balloon flight, so for the demonstration, Étienne put a sheep, a duck, and a rooster in a cage attached to the balloon. The balloon flew almost 2 miles (3 km) before landing, and the animals emerged unharmed.

The test flight with animals seemed to show that balloons could safely and easily transport a person; in November, the first manned hot air balloon flight took place. While in Paris, Étienne had been conducting test flights using balloons that had been tethered to the ground with ropes, and he had gone up in some of these tethered flights himself. Pierre Montgolfier thought ballooning was dangerous, and when he found out about Étienne's test flights, he was so upset that Étienne did not dare pilot the first free flight himself. Two volunteers, Jean-François Pilatre de Rozier and François Laurent, piloted the balloon instead, building the flame up and staying aloft for almost thirty minutes before landing in a field just outside Paris.

Despite the success of that flight, extensive financial support from the French monarchy was not forthcoming. Étienne returned to Vidalon in frustration in 1784. There, he focused on keeping the family business running during the French Revolution of 1789 and the turmoil that followed.

Étienne became involved in politics and held a variety of government positions. By 1799 he was a paymaster for the War Department with an office in Lyon. In late July of that year he

After the creation of hot air balloons, other flying devices, such as the zeppelin (pictured here), took to the skies.

became ill and decided to travel home to Vidalon. He was so unwell, however, that he stopped near the town of Serrières, where he died on August 2, 1799, at the age of fifty-four.

Joseph built another balloon, making a flight himself in Lyon in January 1784. He did not attempt to pursue ballooning further, however, because he became interested in other scientific pursuits, among them designing a parachute and developing a water pump powered by heated air. He also invented the hydraulic ram, a type of water pump that is powered by the energy of the water's own flow.

In 1800, Joseph's many inventions resulted in his being named to the faculty of the Conservatoire National des Arts et Métiers, a technical school in Paris. He worked there until illness forced his retirement in 1809. He died the next year while on a trip to Balaruc-les-Bains in hopes of restoring his health.

The Impact of the Solution on Society

Although the Montgolfiers did not continue ballooning, their pioneering work spurred others to develop new methods of traveling through the air, including passenger balloons, steerable **dirigibles**, and airplanes.

Hot air ballooning quickly fell out of favor. The first manned flight in a balloon filled with hydrogen occurred only a couple of weeks after Rozier and Laurent took a hot air balloon aloft. Since hydrogen ballooning did not require an open flame, it was considered safer than hot air ballooning.

During the nineteenth century and the early twentieth century, hydrogen was widely used in both balloons and other dirigibles such as zeppelins. Hydrogen, however, is quite flammable, and accidents were common. Helium, a nonflammable lighter-than-air gas, was an alternative, but it was expensive.

Finally in 1960, a balloonist named Ed Yost took the next step. He developed a propane burner that could be safely used to generate hot air, creating a modern Montgolfier balloon. Yost's technique caught on, leading both to a revival of hot air ballooning and to the development of recreational ballooning around the world.

Today, hot air balloons continue to fascinate people. In many countries where weather is good and people can get excellent views from above, hot air balloons are used as tourist activities. They may have changed in appearance and mechanics throughout the years, but hot air balloons are still interesting and exciting tools by which people can travel the world.

Timeline

1740
Joseph-Michel Montgolfier born in Vidalon, France

1745
Jacques-Étienne Montgolfier born in Vidalon

1782
Joseph Montgolfier discovers the principle behind hot air ballooning

1783
The Montgolfier brothers hold public demonstrations of their balloons

1799
Étienne Montgolfier dies

1810
Joseph Montgolfier dies

Inventor of the Steam Engine

Thomas Newcomen

1663–1729

Modern society has many machines available to it; however, people may not always appreciate these machines, some of which have been around for centuries. Each machine originated somewhere, and over the years, they evolved into their present states. Some machines have changed entirely but were influential in producing more modern devices. Few know that many of these machines were dependent on the invention of the steam engine in order to be created. Invented by Englishman Thomas Newcomen in the eighteenth century, the steam engine transformed the way people traveled and helped advance society into a modern age.

An Inventor Begins

This image demonstrates Thomas Newcomen's steam engine.

Thomas Newcomen was born in 1663, in Dartmouth, Devon, an important shipping town close to England's southwest coast. The inventor's grandfather, also named Thomas, was a merchant who owned at least one ship and traded with distant lands such as Portugal and Newfoundland in Canada. His son, Elias, inherited some of these shipping interests and also became a merchant. Although the details of Newcomen's early life are incomplete, his family members seem to have been Baptists: they were "**nonconformists**," and so their religious beliefs set them apart from most of their neighbors, who belonged to the Church of England. Historians think Thomas Newcomen may have been taught by John Flavel, a nonconformist scholar from the town of Bromsgrove in the English Midlands, who had moved south to Dartmouth in the 1650s. Flavel seems to have been an important early influence on Newcomen, whose first steam engines would later be built in the Midlands.

For reasons that are unclear, Thomas Newcomen did not become a merchant like his father and grandfather. Instead, in his early twenties, around 1685, he began working as a blacksmith in Dartmouth, selling supplies and tools to the townspeople and helping them to repair equipment. He could not have made much of a living because after his father died in 1702, Newcomen was forced to borrow money from friends and relatives to keep his business going. His partner in this work was John Calley (ca. 1663–1717), whom some historians describe as a plumber and others as a **glazier**; he may have been both. During this time, Newcomen and Calley became aware of a problem that was vexing many people in the West Country and farther afield: how to remove water from mines.

Defining the Problem

Mines are often very deep underground; when coal, tin, and other minerals are removed from them, they fill quickly with water. Unless the water is pumped out, the mines soon become dangerous and impossible to work in. In 1690, a French physicist, Denis Papin (ca. 1647–1712), built a machine for pumping water out of mines. It consisted of a large metal cylinder with a piston. Water was placed inside the cylinder and was then heated by a fire underneath until it turned to steam. The steam expanded, filling the cylinder and raising the piston. The fire was then damped, the cylinder cooled, and the process went into reverse, causing the steam to condense and the piston to fall. Papin used the rising and falling piston to pump water from a mine, but the machine was clumsy and not very good at its task.

After studying Papin's engine, an English army officer, Captain Thomas Savery (ca. 1650–1715), made a much bigger and more ambitious machine that worked in a similar way. He called it an "Engine to Raise Water by Fire" or the "Miner's Friend." In 1698, convinced that he had come up with a winning invention, he took out a patent to register and protect his idea.

Savery, also from the West Country, wrote a book about the Miner's Friend, gave talks on the subject, and opened a factory in London to make the machines. Although Savery's engine worked well, it could raise water only about 20 feet (6 m) and was not very useful in deep mines. Savery had built on Papin's idea of the piston and cylinder and taken them another step, but he still had not solved the problem of pumping water from deep mines. Ultimately the invention was a disappointment, and Savery abandoned it in 1705 after only seven years.

Savery's invention was greeted with great excitement initially. Thus, Newcomen probably had heard about it, especially because the two men lived only 15 miles (24 km) apart. Some historians believe Newcomen was employed by Savery for a time; others think Newcomen was working on his invention at exactly the same time as Savery. No one really knows what made Newcomen and Calley decide to try to make a better pumping engine. Perhaps Savery himself asked for their help, or perhaps Newcomen and Calley saw a Savery engine in action and were inspired to develop something better.

Designing the Solution

Newcomen and Calley soon began to experiment with the same kind of "steam engines" as Papin and Savery. Newcomen started off using drawings of Savery's engine to build small-scale models in his garden. After many experiments, Newcomen found that the best way to improve Savery's engine was to separate the boiler (the part generating the steam) from the cylinder (the part pushing the piston up and down). He decided to seek scientific advice from one of the greatest English scientists of the day, Robert Hooke (1635–1703), who opined that the proposed engine would not work. Like many great inventors, however, Newcomen trusted his own experience

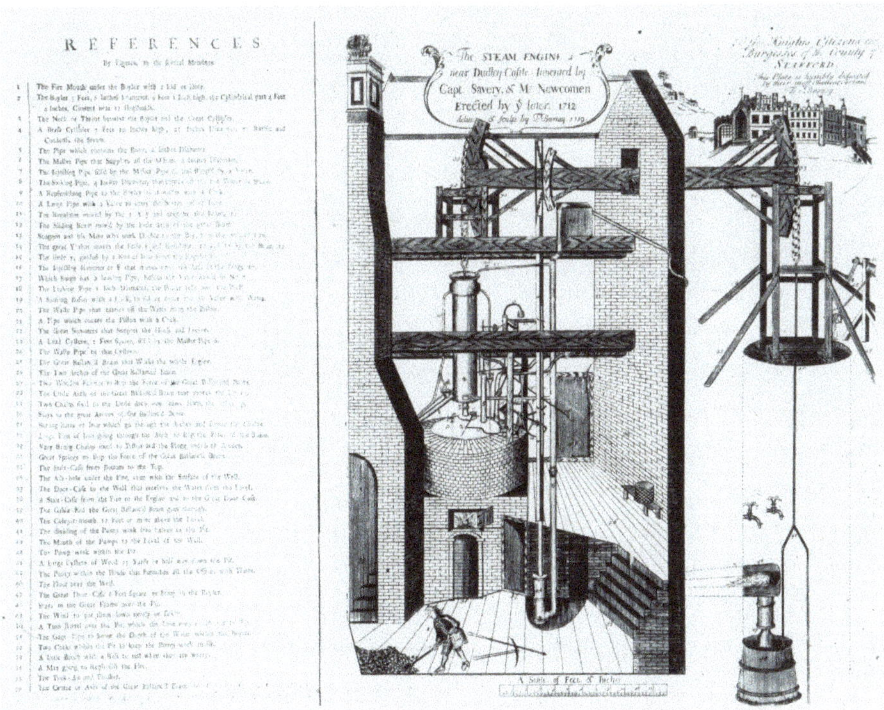

This engraving of the Newcomen steam engine was drawn by Thomas Barney in 1719.

more than the opinions of experts. Even so, Newcomen and Calley needed several years to develop a reliable steam engine.

In 1705, Newcomen and Calley perfected the design of their engine, still working with scale models. Thomas Savery's patent of 1698 would allow him to earn money from any steam-pumping engine similar to the Miner's Friend, so Newcomen had to pay a fee to Savery for each engine he successfully developed.

No one knows when Newcomen built his first full-scale steam engine, although some evidence points to 1710. In 1711, he offered to drain a large coal mine at Griff in the Midlands, where the mine owners were using five hundred horses, at great cost, to pump the

Operating the Steam Engine

All steam engines work in broadly the same way: steam moves a piston back and forth (or up and down) in the cylinder and the moving piston drives another part of the machine to provide useful power. Newcomen's "fire engine," as it was known, was thus really two machines in one.

The main part—the part that Newcomen invented—was a huge steam engine. This was connected by a metal chain to a large wooden beam, rocking up and down, that pumped water up from a coal mine deep below. The steam engine also had two main parts. At the bottom was a large boiler, a bit like a giant kettle. It was filled with water, and a coal fire burned steadily below. Above the boiler was a metal cylinder made of brass or iron with a piston inside it. The piston could rise and fall smoothly inside the cylinder, just like the plunger in a bicycle pump, only much larger: the cylinder was 21 inches (53 cm) in diameter and 7 feet (2 m) high.

Why did Newcomen's engine have to be so gigantic? The power of a steam engine comes from the pressure of the steam inside it, the size of its cylinder, the distance that its piston moves, and how fast it does so. Increasing any one of these increases the engine's power. Newcomen's engine had a large cylinder and a piston that moved a long distance; therefore, it had to be built inside a huge brick building water out. When his offer was turned down, Newcomen made similar offers to other mine owners, including Lord Dudley, who owned mines near his estate in the Midlands.

Dudley accepted the offer, and Newcomen and Calley went to work, building their first major steam engine at a coal mine near Dudley Castle in 1712. Known as the atmospheric engine or fire engine, it was housed in a large brick building on the surface above the mine. A steady supply of coal was needed for the fire to heat the water, which turned into the steam that filled the engine's huge cylinder. As the steam entered and left the cylinder, a piston rose and fell, pushing a beam up and down. The beam was connected to a long rod that passed down a shaft to a pump at the bottom of the mine.

all of its own. Later steam engines used higher-pressure steam and had pistons that moved more quickly, so they could be smaller but also far more powerful than Newcomen's engine.

Newcomen's engine worked in two repeating steps. First, the heavy wooden beam tilted downward, pulling the piston up and opening a valve at the bottom of the cylinder. Steam from the boiler entered the cylinder, filling it completely.

In the second step, the steam valve closed to stop more steam from entering the cylinder, and a water valve on the side of the cylinder opened. A small amount of water from a tank entered the cylinder through the water valve. This cooled the steam inside the cylinder, which made it condense (turn back into water). Water takes up less space than the same amount of steam, so this lowered the pressure inside the cylinder underneath the piston. The air pressure outside the cylinder, which was greater than the pressure inside, pushed the piston down. As the piston fell, it pulled the beam back up. These two steps, in which the piston moved first up and then down again, repeated about twelve times each minute. Each time the beam rose and fell, it pumped 10 gallons (38 liters) of water from the mine to the surface.

As the beam tilted from side to side, it pumped water up from the mine to the surface above.

Historians believe the engine may have taken months to complete. Records seem to show that Newcomen received some help from friends and family members, but he surely would have been in Dudley Castle for much of the time to supervise such an important project. A famous illustration of the engine, made in 1719 by Thomas Barney (see page 83), says that the Dudley Castle engine was jointly invented by "Capt. Savery and Mr. Newcomen," though it is not known whether Savery himself was involved with the Dudley engine.

The Dudley engine was a great success. By 1733, an estimated 110 Newcomen engines had been built throughout Europe. By 1800,

Improving the Steam Engine

Newcomen's steam engine was a great advance on Savery's, but it became much more useful in the hands of James Watt. In 1764, while working at the University of Glasgow in Scotland, Watt was called on to repair a model of one of Newcomen's engines. As he began to study this ingenious machine, he saw much that he could improve. The worst problem was inefficiency: it used an enormous amount of coal. Although coal was always available in the mines where Newcomen's engines were used, the mine owners preferred to sell it instead of using it themselves.

Watt made two big improvements to Newcomen's engine. Newcomen's engine had just a boiler and a cylinder, but Watt's engine had a third part called a condenser. Instead of heating and cooling the cylinder twelve times a minute, thus wasting fuel, Watt kept the cylinder hot all the time and let the steam escape into the separate condenser. In Watt's machine, only the condenser had to be cooled. As a result, his engine used just a quarter of the fuel of Newcomen's and was both smaller and cheaper to run. Watt also figured out how to attach gears to the piston rod so his engine could turn wheels and rotating machinery. This brought steam engines from mines into factories and helped to drive forward the Industrial Revolution.

that number had reached two thousand. From 1755 onward, Newcomen engines were imported into North America. Newcomen did not build all of these machines himself; Calley also constructed some, but most were built by other people who paid Newcomen a license fee to use his idea.

Applying the Solution

Newcomen had to share his profits with Savery so, despite his great success, he kept relatively little of the money he made. Savery had sold shares in his patent to many people, and even after Savery died in 1715, Newcomen still did not keep all his own profits. Historical records suggest that he was trying to invent better kinds of engines in the 1720s, possibly to make up for the money he had paid to Savery and his partners.

In his later years, he seems to have become increasingly active in the Baptist church and may even have been a minister. Newcomen died on August 5, 1729, in London and was buried there the following day. His wife, Hannah, inherited his estate. His three children, who had been born in the years following his marriage in 1705, continued to lead ordinary, modest lives. However, none were to profit from their father's remarkable invention.

Newcomen's engine was practical but inefficient: it used enormous amounts of coal to make its steam. Even so, it remained the most popular way of draining mines for more than fifty years. Just as Newcomen had improved the work of Savery and Papin, a Scots instrument maker named James Watt (1736–1819) used Newcomen's design to make an even better steam engine in 1765. Watt's engine soon found its way into factories to power the machines that drove forward the Industrial Revolution. It sold in great quantities and made Watt very rich. Although Newcomen had done much of the work in making steam engines practical, Watt reaped the rewards.

Soon others had produced even better engines that used steam at higher pressures—accomplished by squeezing the steam into smaller and stronger cylinders, with more powerful and quicker-working pistons. Steam engines had started out as simple machines for pumping water from mines, but small, high-pressure engines were soon being used for other tasks. At the beginning of the nineteenth century, steam engines were driving locomotives, steamships, and large factory machines. By the end of the nineteenth century, they were powering early steam automobiles and generating electricity in power plants. By the beginning of the twentieth century, it seemed the whole world was turned by steam.

The Impact of the Solution on Society

The steam engine was an enormous benefit to society. It changed the way many people functioned. More and more people migrated to cities, looking for work on railways and in factories. The steam engine was a major influence on the Industrial Revolution and changed the world from a largely rural one into a largely industrial one. Thomas Newcomen's invention would be improved upon in later years, but there is little doubt what he created would be written about in history books for centuries.

Timeline

1663
Thomas Newcomen born in Dartmouth, England

1685
Newcomen begins working as a blacksmith

1698
Thomas Savery patents his engine

1705
Newcomen and John Calley build an improved engine

1712
Newcomen and Calley construct their first steam engine at Dudley Castle

1729
Newcomen dies in London

1733
An estimated 110 Newcomen engines are in use across Europe

Inventors of Rollerblades

Brennan Olson and Scott Olson

1963–
and
1959–

In recent decades, there have been inventions created that offer people other modes of transportation. One of these inventions is Rollerblades. Rollerblades are one of the unique objects that have become known by their brand name rather than their product name. In truth, they are a kind of inline skate, but they have become so popular that they are known almost exclusively as Rollerblades, the brand that created this new kind of skate. In the 1980s, brother inventors Brennan and Scott Olson saw a **niche** in the marketplace for a new kind of product. Little did they expect that Rollerblades would influence a generation and even create a new sport based around them.

Scott Olson, one of the coinventors of Rollerblades

Born Brothers

Scott, born in 1959, and Brennan, born in 1963, were two of seven Olson children growing up in St. Louis Park, Minnesota, a suburb of Minneapolis. Like many boys in that part of the United States, they chose ice hockey as their favorite sport.

In 1977, Scott began to play semiprofessional hockey as a goalie for a Winnipeg Jets farm team. Three years later, he stumbled upon a roller skate that would change his life.

Defining the Problem

The story of Rollerblades begins at a sporting-goods store in Bloomington, Minnesota, in 1978. While browsing, Scott discovered an odd-looking pair of roller skates. Unlike most modern roller skates, which had a "quad" or "box" design, with one pair of wheels at the front of the skate and another pair in back, these skates had four wheels in one row down the middle. The front wheel extended beyond the front of the skate and the back wheel extended beyond the rear. They looked remarkably like a pair of ice hockey skates.

In a 1996 interview with the *Wall Street Journal*, Scott said this pair of skates was exactly what he had been imagining for some time. "I immediately fell in love with it," said Scott. "I knew right away what it meant." With a few changes, Scott believed he could make a dry-land hockey skate that could be used outdoors after the spring thaw.

Back in the basement of their parents' home, Scott and Brennan took the frame off the roller skate, swapped the old wheels for new polyurethane ones, added a rubber heel brake, and attached all of it to the boot of a hockey skate. The new skates offered a higher level of control and maneuverability than other roller skates and would allow ice hockey practice year-round. The skates were a hit in the Olsons' circle of hockey-playing friends.

Convinced he had a million-dollar idea on his hands, Scott began to research the patent. He discovered that hundreds of patents had been issued for "inline" skates. The patent for the particular skate he and Brennan had used as their model was originally granted to a company called Super Skate, Inc. Scott negotiated to take over the patent, which had been all but forgotten by the company. US Patent No. 3,880,441 was reassigned to the Olsons and renamed the Super Street Skate.

Designing the Solution

Outside hockey-playing circles, the Olsons' inline skate did not make much of an impact. The brothers took their product door-to-door and were often laughed off the porch. Nevertheless, they believed they were on to something. With no financial backing, they began to advertise their product the only way they could—by skating around town. In 1980, Scott skated 200 miles (322 km) across Minnesota, from Minneapolis to Grand Rapids. Brennan recalls skating with hockey sticks, even when not practicing, "to discourage people from running us off the street."

Applying the Solution

The skates did catch on, largely by word of mouth. Encouraged, Scott founded North American Sports Training Corporation in 1983, backed by private investors. The first mass-produced skates were bulky, heavy, awkward, and unattractive; they were difficult to put on, and the brakes were ineffective.

Brennan was responsible for many of the innovations. He developed a more comfortable, flexible boot; better wheels; and longer-lasting brakes. Subsequent models—most notably the Lightning TRS—were what ensured the Olsons' success. The company was also helped by celebrities such as Wayne Gretzky and Bruce Springsteen, who wore the skates.

In 1984, Scott found himself short of funds. He was forced to sell the company to Minneapolis businessman, billboard magnate, and entrepreneur Robert Naegele Jr. By December 1985, Scott had resigned as president of the company, which had been renamed Rollerblade, Inc. It was not an amicable departure. "[Naegele] took my company," Scott told *Inc.* magazine in 1989. "He outfoxed me." Brennan remained on as director of research and development.

The new president helped switch the focus of the company from young hockey players to a much broader, mainstream audience. Rollerblade, Inc. began marketing Rollerblades throughout Southern California, where there was a well-established skateboarding culture and year-round sunshine. Sales began to boom.

Toward the end of the 1980s, competitors began to emerge in the inline skate market, but because Rollerblade, Inc. had created the market, the new skates were referred to, erroneously, as Rollerblades. By 1991, the sport had grown to such a degree that a group of inline skate manufacturers, retailers, and skaters founded the International Inline Skating Association (IISA). By then, a cottage

A Not So Modern Invention

Inline skates had existed for more than two hundred years before the Olsons invented Rollerblades. As early as the 1700s, the Dutch had fashioned dry-land skates to get around in the months with no ice on the ground.

The first inline skate was patented in 1819 by a Frenchman. The skate had a wooden sole and three wheels aligned in one row. Even though turning the skate was almost impossible, the inline design reigned for nearly forty years. In 1863, an American, James Plimpton, invented a four-wheeled skate, with one pair of wheels under the toe and another under the heel. This design made turning easier and made skating backward possible. Over the next one hundred years, aided by stronger, lighter materials and by advances in ball bearing and wheel design, Plimpton's skate evolved into the roller skate of today. Inline skates still existed, but their popularity had evaporated until the arrival of Rollerblades.

industry of inline skate designers and manufacturers had sprung up in Minnesota—of the five major inline skate companies, three were located in the Minneapolis area. By 1997, inline skating had become a $1-billion global industry. However, much of the financial success came to other companies, such as K2, Salomon, and Nike. In 2000, Rollerblade, Inc. held only 30 percent of the market.

Rollerblading is popular today, especially in sunny areas like California and Florida.

The Impact of the Solution on Society

Scott Olson was not there to experience the rise and fall of Rollerblade, Inc. After his departure, he developed competing products, including the SwitchIt Skate, which could transform easily from an ice skate to an inline roller skate and back again, and the NuSkate, a symmetrical inline skate that allowed the wheels to be detached and reversed to even out the wear on the wheels. Neither brought Olson success.

For much of the 1990s, he was embroiled in legal disputes with Naegele and the company, Nordica, that later purchased Rollerblade, Inc. In December 2000, a district court upheld a lower court's decision to award $4.8 million to Olson in lost royalties from foreign sales.

Scott Olson continued to invent. In addition to new types of inline skates, he created the Rollerbag, a golf bag that becomes its own cart, and life-size plastic lawn penguins that "waddle" in the wind. Olson's most successful follow-up to Rollerblades is the Rowbike, invented in 1993. A Rowbike is a bicycle and rowing machine in one. It has earned praise from *Sports Illustrated* and *Shape* magazines.

Brennan left Rollerblade, Inc. in 1999, when the parent company, Benetton, closed the company headquarters in Minnesota. By then, he had accumulated more than 130 patents.

Neither of the Olson brothers is still officially associated with Rollerblade, Inc., but their names will forever be tied to the product. Their invention started a trend for many children growing up in the 1980s, 1990s, and the twenty-first century. Rollerblades continue to be popular, among children and young adults especially, and you can often see people rollerblading in city parks or near warm beaches. It is clear these products will always have a place in transportation history.

Timeline

1959
Scott Olson born in St. Louis Park, Minnesota

1963
Brennan Olson born in St. Louis Park

1978
The Olson brothers begin to construct inline roller skates

1983
Scott Olson founds the North American Sports Training Corp

1985
Scott Olson resigns as president, while Brennan Olson stays on as director of research and development

1993
Scott Olson invents the Rowbike

1999
Brennan Olson leaves Rollerblade

Inventor of the Modern Helicopter

Igor Sikorsky

1889–1972

Today there are many ways to travel above the clouds: airplanes, rockets, and helicopters. One of the most significant advances in air travel was developed in 1939 by Russian engineer Igor Sikorsky. His version of the modern-day helicopter would give people another option in air travel, one that would persist to this day.

Defining the Problem

Born in Kiev, in what is now Ukraine on May 25, 1889, Igor Ivanovich Sikorsky dreamed of flying even as a boy. At the age of ten, several years before Wilbur and Orville Wright made the first engine-powered airplane in 1903, Sikorsky dreamed that he was inside a luxurious, wood-paneled flying machine. Two years

Igor Sikorsky inside the frame of a helicopter

later, he built himself a small model helicopter powered by a rubber band. Soon he made a better one that could rise several feet into the air. Inspired by other great dreamers, he knew he would fly one day. He was captivated by the stories of French writer Jules Verne (1828–1905) and by the drawings of Italian artist Leonardo da Vinci (1452–1519), who sketched helicopter-like machines in his notebooks around 1483. Sikorsky had been born into a wealthy and well-educated family, and his parents encouraged their son's curiosity.

By the age of fourteen, he was ready to enter the naval academy in Saint Petersburg. Originally, Sikorsky thought he would become a naval officer, but he was much more interested in engineering. Three years later, he quit the academy to study science and math at the Kiev Polytechnic Institute. However, after just one year, frustrated with academics, he abandoned his studies. During a trip to France in 1908, Sikorsky met Wilbur Wright, who was causing a sensation demonstrating his airplane to the French people. It was the first time Europeans had seen an airplane, and Sikorsky was caught up in the general mood of wonder and amazement.

Designing the Solution

When Sikorsky returned to Kiev, he started designing a machine with a spinning rotor that could take off straight up and thus did not need a runway. Using a rotor instead of wings was not a new idea. Chinese inventors had developed a flying top, powered by a spinning feather, around 320 CE. By 1784, two Frenchmen, M. Launoy and M. Bienvenu, had gone one better: they built a model helicopter that flew successfully using two spinning feathers. George Cayley (1773–1857), a British air pioneer, designed a steam-powered helicopter in 1843, but it was too heavy and clumsy to fly. Finally, in 1907, two French inventors managed to lift a person off the ground in primitive helicopters. Louis Breguet (1880–1955) was first in the air: he built a four-rotor helicopter or "gyroplane" that rose about 2 feet (0.6 m) off the ground for a minute or so. Later that year, Paul Cornu (1881–1944) flew a two-rotor machine about 6 feet (1.8 m) off the ground for twenty seconds.

In 1909, at age nineteen, Sikorsky joined the ranks of these helicopter pioneers. Borrowing money from his sister Olga, he traveled to Paris, where most of the early aviators were based. As he began meeting people, he learned what he could about building planes and bought a small airplane engine. When he returned to Kiev, he used it to build a crude two-rotor helicopter. The basic idea worked well: the rotors could generate lift (upward force), but not enough to raise the craft off the ground. The following year, Sikorsky tried a bigger engine but still failed to fly. After these two disappointments, he realized he was too short of money, experience, and materials to make a helicopter at that time.

Instead, Sikorsky decided to try making ordinary airplanes. In 1910, he built a biplane (an airplane with two wings, one above the other) called the S-1, which also failed to fly. He was more successful with his next planes—the S-2 through S-4—and by 1911 his S-5 could stay in the air more than an hour at an **altitude** of 1,480 feet (451 m). Sikorsky's father paid for these early adventures and even mortgaged the family home to help. His faith in his son was repaid in 1912, when Sikorsky won first prize at an air exhibition in Moscow. The same year, Sikorsky won backing from the Russian Baltic Railroad Car Factory, for which he became chief aircraft engineer.

Between 1912 and the end of World War I in 1918, Sikorsky designed and built some of the best airplanes in Russia. His S-21, also known as the Grand, was a luxurious, four-engine plane, the first to have an enclosed cabin for the passengers and crew; it even had a dining table, a sofa, and a bathroom. Later, Sikorsky made a military version of the Grand that could carry bombs. This important contribution to the Russian war effort earned him an engraved gold watch presented personally by the **czar**.

Applying the Solution

In 1918, the Bolshevik Revolution threw Russia into turmoil. People like Sikorsky, who had become rich and famous, were targets for the Bolsheviks, who believed that money and property should be shared more equally. With a single suitcase and a small amount of money in his pocket, Sikorsky fled Russia. After visiting France briefly, he left for the United States, arriving in New York City on March 30, 1919.

Sikorsky's passport noted that he planned to build aircraft, but no one in the United States was interested; many surplus warplanes were available at discount prices. Instead he took a temporary job with the US Army Air Service in Dayton, Ohio. Later he became a math teacher on New York City's Lower East Side, living in one small room

A Helicopter in Action

A helicopter flies in a completely different way from an airplane. Its huge spinning rotor provides both its lifting power and its steering. The rotor is an immensely complicated mechanical system made up of many levers and gears, mounted on top of a powerful engine. The rotor has several spinning blades, each with a straight undersurface and a curved top edge, like the airfoil wing of an airplane. As the rotor spins, the blades chop through the air several hundred times each minute. This makes an upward force called lift that balances the helicopter's weight and keeps it in the air. As Sikorsky said, "The helicopter approaches closer than any other vehicle to fulfillment of mankind's ancient dreams of the flying horse and the magic carpet."

Using a control stick—the collective pitch—the pilot can tilt the rotor blades to a different angle (pitch) to suit different stages of flying. During takeoff, the pilot sets the blades to a steep angle so that they will generate a huge amount of lift. The lift force exceeds the craft's weight, so the helicopter rises. During landing, the pilot sets the blades to a shallow angle so that the weight exceeds the rotor lift and the helicopter lowers to the ground. For hovering in midair, the pilot sets the pitch so that the upward lift exactly balances the helicopter's weight.

in Manhattan. Now age thirty, he had lost his money, his fame, his homeland, and his job, but he continued to dream of building a helicopter.

Fortunately, many other Russians had fled to the United States, and some agreed to help Sikorsky restart his business. Within four years, he set up the Sikorsky Aero Engineering Company in an old barn at a farm on Roosevelt Field, Long Island. Soon renamed the Sikorsky Manufacturing Corporation, the company made successful passenger airplanes and, later, flying boats ("Clippers"), which opened up passenger routes to the Caribbean and South America for Pan-American Airways. The 1920s brought an upturn in Sikorsky's fortunes. He married his wife Elizabeth in 1924, and four years later he became an American citizen. The following year, 1929, his company was taken over by the United Aircraft Corporation, which opened a large new plant in Connecticut.

Rotor blades also control how a helicopter steers. Using a second control stick called the cyclical pitch, the pilot can set the blades so they change from a steep to a shallow angle, and back again, every time they rotate. To go forward, the pilot adjusts the cyclical pitch so each blade makes a steep angle when it is at the back of the helicopter and a shallow angle at the front. The blades generate more lift at the back of the craft than at the front, so the nose tilts down and the helicopter flies forward. The pilot can make the helicopter fly in other directions by tilting the blades in other ways.

With only one rotor, a helicopter's entire body tends to spin around. Some helicopters have two rotors that **counter-rotate** to control this spin. Sometimes the two rotors are at opposite ends of the body, as on the giant military Chinook helicopter. Sometimes the rotors turn in opposite ways on the same shaft. Igor Sikorsky discovered that it was possible to build a helicopter with only one rotor provided he added a smaller rotor, mounted vertically on the tail, which balances the turning effect of the main rotor. This tail rotor may look small and unimportant, but the helicopter cannot fly safely without it.

Although his companies in Russia and the United States had concentrated on making airplanes, Sikorsky was still thinking about how to build a helicopter. Since his early efforts in 1909 and 1910, European engineers had made great advances. In 1916, two Austrians, professor Theodor von Kármán (1881–1963) and Lieutenant Stefan Petroczy, had flown a crude helicopter to 600 feet (183 m) for an hour, though it carried no passengers and was tied to the ground with safety cables. Seven years later, Spaniard Juan de la Cierva (1895–1936) built his autogyro, a one-person airplane with small wings and a helicopter rotor on top.

"If a man is in need of rescue, an airplane can come in and throw flowers on him, and that's just about all. But a direct lift aircraft could come in and save his life."
—Igor Sikorsky

Helicopters finally became practical in the 1930s. All the work that airline pioneers had done with fixed-wing airplanes made it easier for them to understand how helicopters behaved in the air. Engines and materials had also improved. Sikorsky had developed much of the theory behind the helicopter, patenting his ideas on June 27, 1931. However, he needed almost another decade to get the machine into the sky. European rivals surged ahead: in France, Louis Breguet made a two-rotor helicopter that was flying at 500 feet (152 m) by 1935. Two years later, in Germany, Heinrich Focke (1890–1979) built another twin-rotor helicopter that reached altitudes of 8,000 feet (2,438 m) and stayed at that height for more than an hour. Finally, in 1939, Sikorsky started to build his own machine. Unlike the European aircraft designers, he opted for a much simpler design using a single rotor blade because, as he explained, "One person in the kitchen is fine. Two people in the kitchen get in each other's way."

Sikorsky was known for always making the first test flight in his own airplanes; he was also known for his impeccable dress. Thus, on September 14, 1939, wearing a dark suit and fedora hat, Sikorsky climbed into the pilot's seat of his VS-300 helicopter, switched on the rotor, and took off. Made of welded steel tubes, with a 75-horsepower engine and a single three-blade rotor, Sikorsky's helicopter was simply built but alarming to fly. On its maiden voyage, Sikorsky said it lurched to one side "like a frightened horse." The early days of testing saw several crashes and nineteen major redesigns, but improvements came quickly. By 1940, the machine could fly for fifteen minutes at a time, and in 1943, the world's first practical single-rotor helicopter went into full-scale production.

On May 6, 1941, Sikorsky set a world record, staying in the air at treetop height for 1 hour, 32 minutes, 26 seconds. The following year, he delivered a version of his S-47 helicopter (also known as the XR-4) to the US Army Air Corps. During World War II and the Korean War, Sikorsky helicopters, including the S-51 (the military version was known as R-5), proved their worth in medical, search and rescue, and combat missions. From the 1950s onward, new developments such as the jet engine allowed helicopters to fly farther and faster, and to carry greater loads.

Since Sikorsky's VS-300 took to the air in 1939, helicopters have repeatedly proved their worth, saving thousands of lives in famines, floods, fires, and other challenging situations. In almost every conflict since World War II, helicopters have served as versatile attack aircraft and air ambulances. In peacetime, they have helped with everything from geological surveys to cattle ranching. Their enormous flexibility comes from their ability to take off or land vertically, hover or rotate around one spot, or drift very slowly in any direction—maneuvers no ordinary airplane can do.

The Impact of the Solution on Society

Sikorsky worked for his company as aircraft designer and engineering manager. He continued to improve his helicopters and filed more patents, mainly concerned with better ways of steering and controlling his aircraft. Even after he retired in 1957 at age sixty-eight, the company kept him on as a part-time consultant. Sikorsky always commanded people's immediate respect because of his thorough knowledge of his subject. A quiet, gentle, and polite man who greeted everyone with a bow, he was said never to raise his voice and never to lose his temper.

Retirement gave him time for other interests. A refined and educated man, he wrote religious and philosophical books and helped to construct an Orthodox church for the Russian community near Bridgeport, Connecticut. He also loved the drama of the natural world: he was a keen amateur astronomer and would fly thousands of miles to watch volcanoes erupting. He died at age eighty-three at his family home, a farmhouse in Easton, Connecticut, on October 26, 1972.

Today Sikorsky's single-rotor helicopters are still used. Helicopters themselves have become important tools in transporting people from places such as oilrigs, in times of emergency, and for medical procedures. Although Sikorsky was not the first to invent the helicopter, his design influenced society and thrived.

Timeline

1889
Igor Ivanovich Sikorsky born in Kiev, Ukraine

1909
Sikorsky learns about building airplanes in Paris

1910
Sikorsky builds the S-1 through S-4 biplanes

1912
Sikorsky becomes chief aircraft engineer for the Russian Baltic Railroad Car Factory

1919
Sikorsky arrives in the United States

1923
Sikorsky sets up the Sikorsky Manufacturing Corporation

1931
Sikorsky patents his theories behind the helicopter

1939
Sikorsky begins to build his own helicopter

1943
The first practical single-rotor helicopter goes into full-scale production

1957
Sikorsky retires

1972
Sikorsky dies

Pioneer of Railroads

George Stephenson

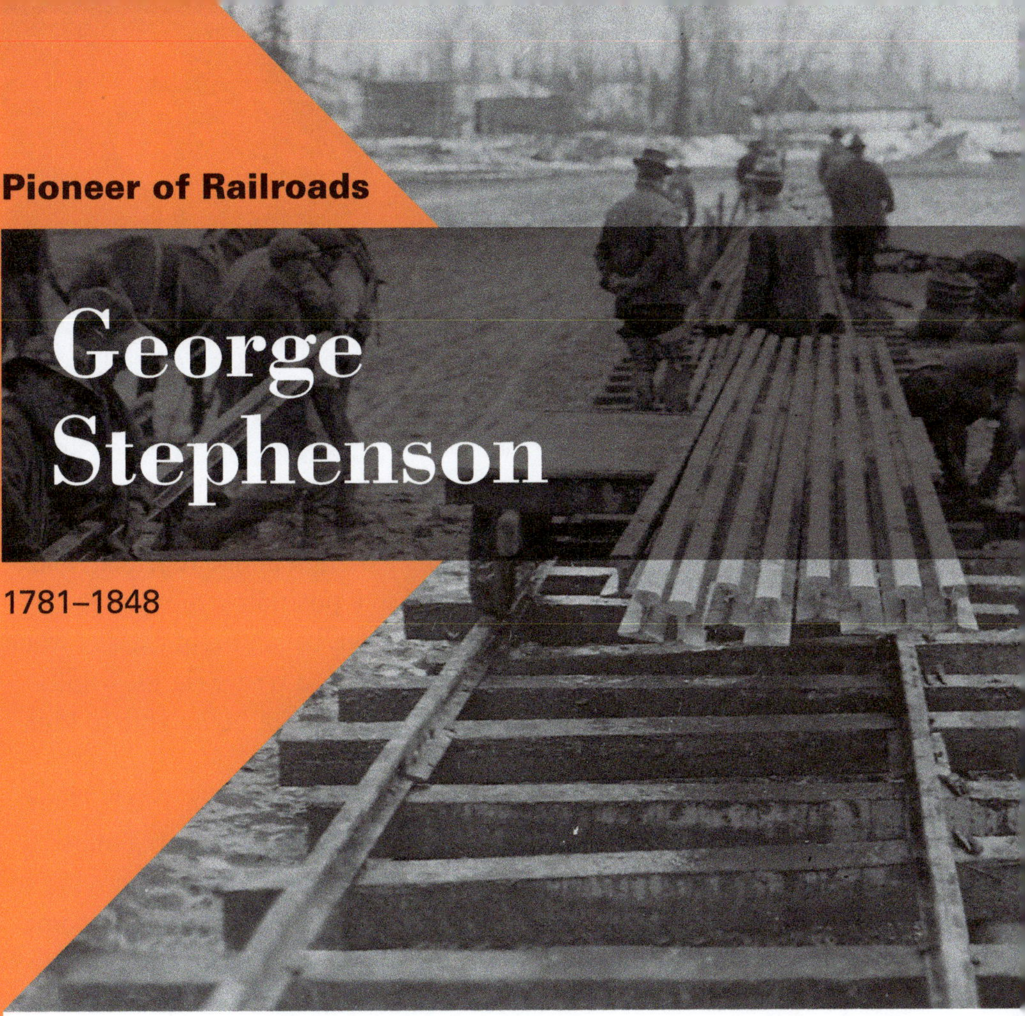

1781–1848

Every so often there comes an invention that truly changes the world. In the 1800s, British engineer George Stephenson contributed to changing the world around him with his designs for locomotives. His influence resulted in locomotive rail networks all over the planet. Travel by rail became so popular that it opened new avenues for pioneers in America, allowing people to spread into territory out west. Over time, trains and railroads became monumental, and today they continue to exist as ways of transporting goods and people across long distances.

Youth and Invention

George Stephenson

George Stephenson was born in the coal-mining village of Wylam in northern England on June 9, 1781. His father helped operate a steam engine used for pumping water out of the local coal mine. The family was poor, and neither George nor his five brothers and sisters went to school.

George grew up with a great interest in engines, became his father's assistant at age fourteen, and within a couple of years was promoted to a position senior to his father. Wanting to become educated, George began night classes when he was eighteen, only then learning to read and write. He grew into a strong, confident young man with a reputation of being able to look after himself.

George married a local farmer's daughter, Fanny, in 1802. Their only son, Robert, also became a famous railroad engineer. Times were hard in Britain economically, and George considered moving to North America, but he persevered at home. By 1812, he had become a senior engineer, in charge of all the engines at his local coal mine. He also worked on other projects—for example, inventing a safety lamp that miners could use underground without the risk of setting off gas explosions. In 1814, he took up a new challenge, one that other local engineers had also recently attempted: he built his first railroad locomotive.

Defining the Problem

Railroads had existed for centuries before George Stephenson was born. In mining areas, owners would lay wooden or iron rails across the ground so that horses could pull trucks to the nearest river or canal. One such track ran in front of George's childhood home.

The idea of building a steam locomotive to run on rails came much later. The first practical steam engine was constructed in 1712 by British inventor Thomas Newcomen (1664–1729); it was a huge machine used for pumping water out of mine shafts. However, these early steam engines used steam only at low pressure. Thus, they were not powerful enough to push themselves along in the way that a locomotive could.

High-pressure steam engines were the answer, but they were difficult to build with the technology of the time, and the danger that the water boiler in the steam engine would explode was always present. British inventor James Watt (1736–1819) who improved Newcomen's engines, thought high-pressure steam would be too dangerous. His influence delayed the development of high-pressure steam engines in Britain.

The first steam engine that moved under its own power using high-pressure steam was built in France in 1769. It was designed for road travel rather than railroads and was clumsy and impractical. Finally, in 1804, British engineer Richard Trevithick (1771–1833) built the first railroad locomotive; a Trevithick locomotive successfully pulled trucks at a coal mine. Trevithick's work proved that a locomotive with smooth wheels, running on smooth track, would still have enough "grip" to pull a train. However, the rails themselves tended to break under the engine's weight, and Trevithick also could not demonstrate decisively that his engines would be cheaper than horses. Discouraged, he abandoned locomotive development around 1808 and turned to other projects.

Soon, economic changes in Britain helped turn people's minds toward locomotives again. The country was at war with France, horses were in short supply, and the price of their fodder (food) rose. At a coal mine, on the other hand, the coal fuel for powering locomotives was virtually free. Around 1812, a few engineers at British coal mines started constructing their own locomotives, using and improving upon Trevithick's designs.

Designing the Solution

George Stephenson built his first locomotive in 1814. He built others, continuously improving the designs, and he soon gained a reputation as the best locomotive engineer in Britain. All his earliest locomotives, however, were slow-moving machines built for owners of coal mines. The idea of public railroads that could crisscross the country, carrying people and freight, was still distant. One or two British writers had published their ideas for a national railroad network, but they were not taken seriously at first, especially as another transportation network—the canals—had only just been created.

What turned out to be a decisive step was taken by the merchants in the town of Darlington, in northern England, in 1818. They started planning a railroad that, although only 25 miles (40 km) long, would be the longest in the world at that time. It would run from nearby coal mines via Darlington to the seaport town of Stockton. This was to be a public railroad that anyone could pay to use—passengers as well as commercial firms.

George Stephenson was appointed engineer to the Stockton and Darlington Railway in 1822, responsible for all aspects of the work, including laying track and building bridges. He got the directors' permission to build the track strong enough to support locomotives and horses (the original plan was to have horses pull the train cars). The challenges Stephenson faced were not just technical. A special

The Locomotive

The steam locomotives that hauled mainline trains well into the twentieth century all traced their ancestry back to Rocket, the engine designed and built by George Stephenson, his son Robert, and their assistants in 1829. Rocket was not the first locomotive, but it was the first fast, efficient design for one. Although later locomotives were built much bigger, they all worked in fundamentally the same way.

The basic design of a steam locomotive, whether Rocket or a later model, began with a firebox or furnace at the back, into which a driver's assistant, called a "fireman," shoveled fuel. The hot gases from the fire traveled in metal pipes called "fire tubes" through the cylindrical water boiler that formed the main body of the locomotive. Some of the heat in the gases transferred across the pipes to the water, causing it to boil and producing steam at high pressure. The gases from the fire then passed out of the fire tubes and up the chimney. Rocket was the first locomotive to have many small fire tubes, rather than just one or two large ones. This design transferred law had to be passed by the British Parliament to allow the line to be built, and difficult negotiations were entered into with landowners who did not want the railroad to cross their land. The line finally opened on September 27, 1825, with great ceremony and with Stephenson's engine, Locomotion, pulling a train of thirty-three cars and trucks, carrying hundreds of passengers as well as freight.

Passengers were only a minor part of the Stockton and Darlington Railway, and their cars were pulled by horses on normal days. Stephenson had now begun working as engineer on a much bigger project—the world's first mainline railroad, planned to run between the major cities of Liverpool and Manchester in England, where passengers were to be important from the beginning. Difficulties again arose with the British Parliament and with landowners, as well as with canal owners who did not want competition.

Locomotives still had to prove themselves to many doubters. For example, some directors of the new railroad thought that pulling cars on ropes using large stationary steam engines would work better. To see whether faster, better locomotives could be produced, the

heat to the water much more efficiently, a major factor that aided its victory in the locomotive competition in 1829. Since then, all steam locomotives have been built with multiple fire tubes.

To move a locomotive such as Rocket, high-pressure steam flowed in pipes from the boiler to two hollow piston-containing cylinders, one on each side of the vehicle. The force of the steam, directed by automatic valves, pushed the pistons first one way and then the other. A rod on each piston linked to other rods that forced the "driving wheels" (the front wheels in Rocket's case) to rotate. The amount of steam reaching the cylinders and thus the speed and power of the locomotive were controlled by the driver. After leaving the cylinders, "waste" steam was directed up the chimney, which also helped draw hot gases from the fire through the fire tubes, increasing efficiency. Other features that Rocket shared with later locomotives included safety valves on the boiler, control levers to put the locomotive into reverse, and springs for a smoother ride.

directors organized a trial in 1829 in which a large prize was offered for the best locomotive. This trial was easily won by Rocket, built by a firm run by George Stephenson and his son Robert and driven by George Stephenson himself. The following year the Liverpool and Manchester Railway opened to the public and was a huge success. The railroad era had begun.

Applying the Solution

Now that railroads had proved successful, suddenly everyone wanted to build them, in Britain and abroad. George Stephenson had plenty of work offered to him, although nothing he did later was as important historically as his first two railroads. Stephenson had a widespread reputation as a stubborn man, and some railroad firms preferred to use other engineers, including his own former assistants.

During the 1830s, Stephenson became a rich mine owner as well as an engineer, taking advantage of new coalfields he had discovered while digging excavations for his railroads. He bought land and a large house and took up hothouse gardening, then newly fashionable. He even competed successfully with an aristocratic neighbor in

George's Son

George Stephenson's son Robert (1803–1859) was only nineteen when he began to run the locomotive works established jointly by his father and local businessmen. Better educated than his father, Robert was also different in character—known among his peers as being more willing to give credit to other people. Robert and his father worked well together, however, and later Robert supervised large railroad projects of his own.

Most notably, Robert pioneered large and daring designs for railroad bridges, including a massive bridge over the Saint Lawrence River at Montreal. Although George Stephenson is better known in modern times, Robert was quite famous during his lifetime and was given the rare honor (for an engineer) of being buried in London's Westminster Abbey.

Today, locomotives are still used to transport goods and people from place to place.

attempts to grow a straight cucumber. In his last years, George Stephenson was a celebrity, touring England to give talks about his early life. He died in 1848.

The Impact of the Solution on Society

It is difficult to overstate the changes that railroads brought to society. Developed in an era before automobiles, trucks, or airplanes, they amazed people with the speed at which they could transport passengers and freight. Many aspects of everyday life changed. City dwellers, for example, could choose to live in the country, traveling to work every day by train. Railroads also opened up remote areas to new human settlement.

The first locomotive in the United States was imported from Britain in 1829, but domestically built models soon became commonplace. The US railroad network expanded rapidly. The Civil War (1861–1865) has been described as the first railroad war, with rail networks playing an important role in transporting troops and supplies. A landmark came in 1869, when railroads were built from the west and the east, meeting in Utah to complete the first transcontinental line. By the end of the nineteenth century, more than 200,000 miles (321,867 km) of railroad track wove across the United States.

Steam locomotives remained the main power units on the world's railroads until around the middle of the twentieth century. (The world's largest locomotives, the Union Pacific's "Big Boys," were built as late as the 1940s.) Though powerful, steam locomotives needed careful maintenance and were very wasteful of fuel. Contemporary locomotives are either diesel-powered or electric, and thus are more efficient.

Even though the importance of rail travel has diminished over time, particularly in the United States, railroads continue to be symbols of expansion and opportunities for safe, more efficient travel. In many countries in Europe, train travel is popular, allowing citizens to commute without hassle of traffic on roads. Likewise, train travel pollutes less and results in fewer accidents. Because of Stephenson's influence, the locomotive and railroad have continued to have importance in modern society.

Timeline

1781
George Stephenson born in Wylam, England

1812
Stephenson becomes a senior engineer at a local coal mine

1814
Stephenson builds his first locomotive

1822
Stephenson is appointed engineer to the Stockton and Darlington Railway

1825
Stephenson's engine Locomotion opens the Stockton and Darlington Railway

1829
Stephenson's Rocket wins a prize for best locomotive

1848
Stephenson dies

Pioneer of Radar

Robert Watson-Watt

1892–1973

Throughout decades, technological advancement has often arrived as a result of war or conflict. Some of the world's most significant inventions have likewise arisen during times of strife. During World War II, many inventions were created in an effort to preserve and protect life and defeat the enemy. One such invention was radar, developed by Scottish scientist Robert Watson-Watt and used today for many purposes.

Drawn to Invention

Robert Watson-Watt was born on April 13, 1892, in the town of Brechin, Aberdeenshire, in Scotland. His father was a carpenter, as his grandfather had been. His mother was a

Sir Robert Watson-Watt on board the *Queen Elizabeth* in 1951

passionate feminist and was also active in temperance reform, a worldwide movement that tried to reduce widespread alcohol abuse in the nineteenth century.

After attending a local school in Brechin, Watson-Watt went to the University of Dundee to study electrical engineering. It was a new and exciting field, particularly since the Italian inventor Guglielmo Marconi (1874–1937) had recently made the first practical demonstrations of radio. After Watson-Watt graduated in 1912, he became an assistant to William Peddie, who encouraged him to study radio. In 1915, Watson-Watt moved to the south of England to work for the British government's Meteorological (Met) Office. There, he began to develop radio equipment that could be used to detect incoming thunderstorms. He was granted his first patent for a radio-detecting device in 1919.

Defining the Problem

Watson-Watt did not invent the idea of detecting objects by the use of radio waves. Like radio itself, this invention resulted from many different people's efforts. For example, British physicist James Clerk Maxwell (1831–1879) set out the basic science of radio in 1873. A German physicist named Heinrich Hertz (1857–1894) made the first radio waves in his laboratory some years later. The first person to try to detect objects with radio waves was another German, Christian Hulsmeyer (1881–1957). In 1904, he patented the telemobiloscope, a radio device that ships could use to locate one another. The German navy had little interest, however, and the device was never manufactured.

The first real demonstration of the power of radio detection came from scientists who were trying to understand Earth's atmosphere. Marconi had demonstrated that radio waves could travel immense distances around the curved Earth, something many had thought impossible. Scientists believed that Earth's atmosphere was responsible: they thought it was bending radio waves around the planet's curved surface, a bit like a mirror in space. In 1924, English scientist Edward Appleton (1892–1965) fired radio waves into the atmosphere to prove this hypothesis; Gregory Breit (1899–1981) and Merle Tuve (1901–1982) conducted a similar experiment in the United States in 1925. These scientists timed how long the radio waves took to return and so proved the existence of the ionosphere, the part of the atmosphere that bends radio waves around Earth. These experiments were the first successful use of radio detection.

While this pioneering work was under way, Watson-Watt was still working in the Meteorological Office. In 1927, following a government reorganization, his department was merged with another to form the Radio Research Station, and Watson-Watt was put in charge. He was a popular and enthusiastic boss who respected the scientists who were working for him. Teamwork proved vital in the development of radar.

During the 1930s, Germany was enlarging its military forces at a rate that alarmed other European nations, who feared attack. In 1934, Britain conducted a mock air raid on its capital city, London, to see how easily enemy bombers could reach it. Even with air defenses in place, more than half the mock bombers found their targets. Around the same time, rumors reached England that the German leader, Adolf Hitler, was developing a "death ray": an invisible, high-powered beam of radio waves that could be fired from an airplane to obliterate an entire city. Watson-Watt was asked to advise the British government about whether this was possible. His assistant, Arnold F. Wilkins, quickly calculated that radio waves were much too weak for such use. However, Wilkins and Watson-Watt realized that radio beams did have important military potential—as air defense.

Designing the Solution

On February 26, 1935, they built a primitive test system using a British Broadcasting Company (BBC) radio transmitter and showed that it could detect a bomber up to 8 miles (13 km) away. The government awarded them £10,000 for further research (equivalent to almost $170,000 US in 2014), and they built a research station on the east coast of England at Orford Ness. By June of that year, their Radio Direction Finding (RDF) system, as it was then known, could detect ships and planes approaching more than 40 miles (64 km) away—around eleven minutes before they posed a serious threat. Between 1935 and 1939, Watson-Watt and his team built a series of twenty radio detection stations around the south and east coasts of England, named Chain Home. This original network was later doubled in size.

Applying the Solution

By September 1938, Chain Home was operating twenty-four hours a day. When war broke out in 1939, the system proved invaluable in helping Britain defend itself against air attacks from Germany. Watson-Watt's radar research team continued to refine and improve radar apparatus. In 1940, two members of the team, Henry Boot (1917–1983) and John Randall (1905–1984), developed the magnetron, a piece of apparatus that generated radio waves at higher power and frequency. Radio-detecting equipment could now be made smaller and carried more easily on airplanes and ships. Thus it could be used not just to defend against enemy bombers from the ground but also to help British planes aim their own missiles more effectively. The team was thought to be a target for enemy attacks, however. In 1940, it was moved farther out of range of German bombers to a farm in the remote village of Worth Matravers on the south coast. Two years later, it was moved to safety again—this time inland to the Malverns near Wales.

The British were not alone in developing radio detection for military use. They worked closely with scientists in the United States, who found a much snappier name for the invention. They called it radar (radio detecting and ranging) because it used radio waves to locate objects (detecting) and to find out how far away they were (ranging). The US Army developed powerful radar of its own, both for detecting incoming planes and for controlling antiaircraft guns to stop them. Radar like this was installed in Hawaii in 1941 and detected the approach of Japanese airplanes on December 7 shortly before the attack on Pearl Harbor.

Radar, as it was now known, gave Britain and its allies an advantage over Germany. Ironically, the Germans had developed their own version of radar before the war. Confident of victory over Europe, they canceled its development in 1940. During that same time, the British and Americans stepped up their radar research—and reaped the rewards. In the summer of 1940, the Luftwaffe (the German air force) launched a major air attack on England that became known as the Battle of Britain. Using 2,600 airplanes, Germany tried to devastate the British forces in preparation for an invasion. The British had only a quarter as many airplanes. Even so, they won the air battle using radar, which helped them locate and destroy enemy planes much more effectively.

The Basics of Radar

People can see things because light reflects off objects and makes them visible. Light travels 186,000 miles (299,338 km) in a second, so perception happens more or less instantaneously. To see at night, cars shine their headlights into the darkness. Light travels out from the car, hits objects in the distance, and reflects back into the driver's eyes. Headlights are ineffective in airplanes and ships, however, because darkness and bad weather can sometimes prevent pilots from seeing more than a few feet ahead.

Radar is like an invisible headlight that can cut through darkness and bad weather. Inside an airplane the radar transmitter regularly sends out coded signals consisting of radio waves. These are similar to light, and they travel just as quickly, but they pass through darkness and fog and travel much farther. The radio waves continue to travel until they hit something (for example, a nearby helicopter), then bounce back again. The airplane also has a radar receiver that detects incoming radar signals. When it receives the signals, it decodes them and calculates how long they took to travel to the helicopter and return. Knowing that the signals traveled at 186,000 miles (299,338 km) per second, it can figure out how far away the helicopter is and how quickly it is approaching. Pilots can use this information, like a second pair of eyes, to alter course and avoid a collision.

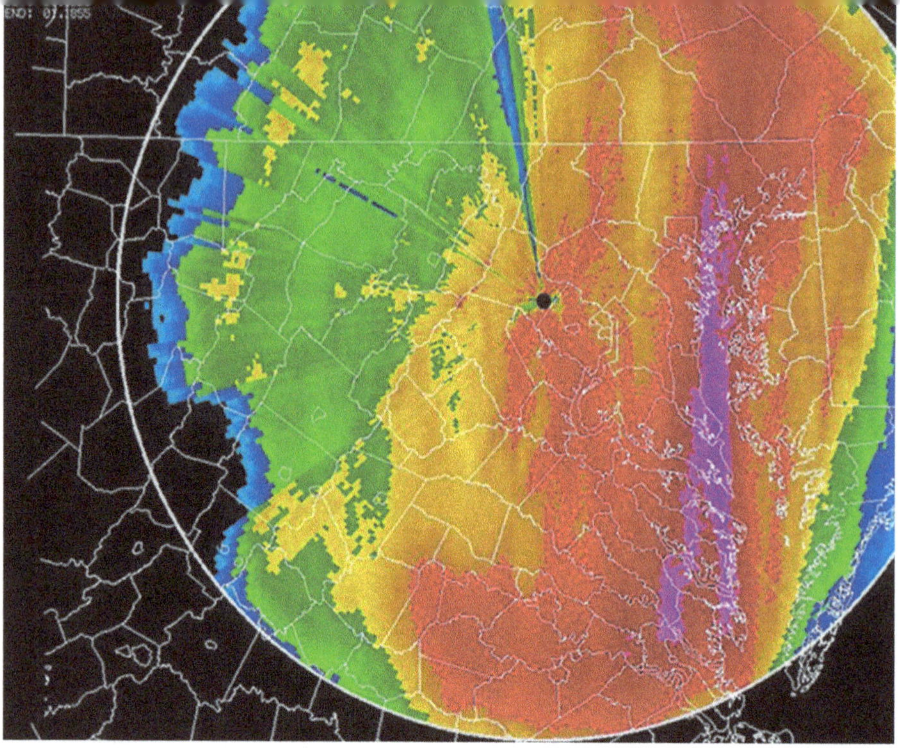

Many services rely on radar, such as Doppler radar, to navigate the weather.

The Impact of the Solution on Society

After World War II ended in 1945, radar continued to find important military applications. For much of the late twentieth century, the world was engaged in the Cold War: the two superpowers (the United States and the former Soviet Union) built up enormous stocks of long-range missiles to use against each other. Large radar installations were established at the same time to warn each side against impending missile attacks from the other.

When jet airplanes became popular in the 1950s, and the skies grew more crowded, radar became essential for navigation. Air-traffic controllers also started using radar to manage the flow of planes into and out of airports. Similarly, harbormasters used radar to steer ships into and out of busy ports, and ships themselves began to find radar invaluable for navigating in bad weather or when visibility was poor. Radar makes air and sea travel considerably safer than it would be if pilots and captains had to rely entirely on what they could see—as was the case in the early twentieth century.

In the modern world, radar has found many uses apart from military detection and navigation. Robert Watson-Watt first used radar technology to help him detect thunderstorms; a type of radio detector, Doppler radar, is one of the most useful tools for weather forecasters today. It can locate advancing storms and determine both the probability of rain's arriving at a certain time and the expected severity of a storm. Police officers use a similar technology in radar speed cameras, which calculate how fast cars are traveling by bouncing a radar beam off them.

Although Robert Watson-Watt was not responsible for creating these modern uses for radar or radio detecting devices, he did prove that radio waves had benefits that could be used on a large scale. He likewise became a foremost expert in radar, and his contributions to science are forever remembered and celebrated. In recognition for his accomplishments, Watson-Watt was knighted in 1942. Ten years later, the British government awarded him £50,000 as a reward for his work. He spent much of his later life in Canada and the United States before returning to his native Scotland. It was there in Inverness, Scotland, that he died, on December 5, 1973, at the age of eighty-one.

Timeline

1892
Robert Watson-Watt born in Brechin, Scotland

1915
Watson-Watt begins working for the Meteorological Office

1927
Watson-Watt is put in charge of the Radio Research Station

1935
Watson-Watt and his team begin building the Chain Home radar system

1942
Watson-Watt is knighted

1973
Watson-Watt dies

Inventor of Devices for Electric Railways

Granville Woods

1856–1910

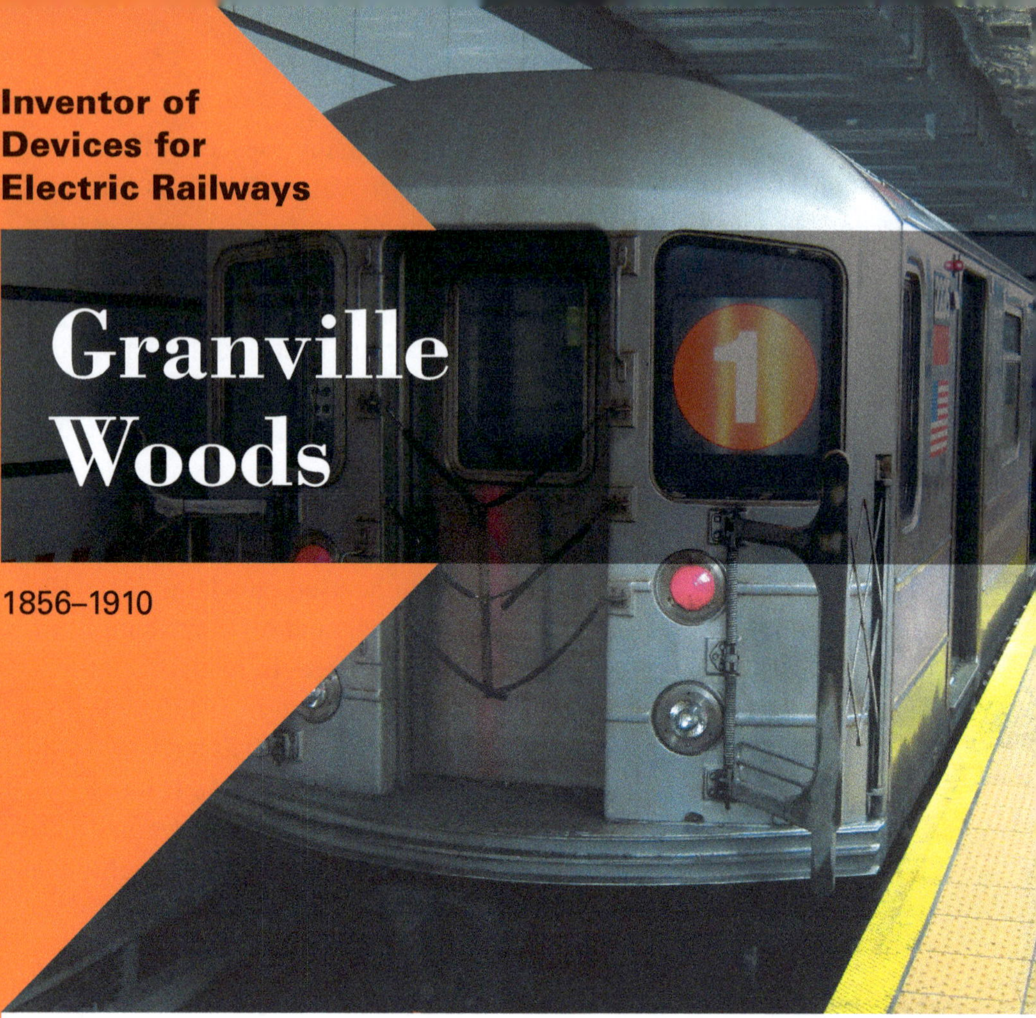

During the late nineteenth century and early twentieth century, the railroad industry was booming. Many people were traveling across the United States, and many others wanted to play a role in designing new and exciting projects for the railroads and similar devices. However, this was also a time where it was very difficult for people—especially African Americans—to gain recognition for their inventions. Such was the case with Granville Woods, a man who had a dream of contributing to the ever-growing train revolution. Despite hardships, and with persistence, determination, and technique, Woods's aspirations became reality.

Granville T. Woods, ca. 1887

Beginnings

Little is known about Granville Woods's early life. Most sources agree that he was born in 1856, but whereas some historians maintain that he was born in Columbus, Ohio, others point to contemporary sources indicating that he was actually born in Australia.

Whatever the case, Woods grew up in Columbus. His family was quite poor, and Woods left school at an early age to work. When Woods was fifteen years old, he took a job as a machinist. A year later, he began studying electricity on his own. For the next few years, he continued to work at technical jobs in several cities.

Defining the Problem

Sometime in the mid-1870s, Woods moved to the East Coast (the exact location remains unknown). There, he was finally able to obtain a more formal education, studying mechanical engineering at a technical school for two years. In the late 1870s, Woods returned to Ohio to work for the many railroads there. While at the railroads, Woods became interested in learning to use the telegraph.

Woods also developed an interest in elevators; he decided that the method then in use of communicating between the elevator car and the floors was inadequate. Woods quit the railroads and went to work developing his new elevator-communication system. When he showed his invention to a patent attorney, he was told that it would probably not catch on because of the cost.

Woods decided to develop his **induction** system for use in railroads. In the summer of 1881, however, he contracted smallpox, a potentially fatal disease that left him unable to work for almost a year.

Woods recovered physically, but the illness left him penniless. He began looking for a financial backer for his induction idea and other inventions. In 1883, Woods was able to obtain money from a backer to patent a steam boiler; the next year, he patented an improved telephone transmitter. That year he also patented a device for voice communication over telegraph lines. Woods's patent was eventually purchased by American Bell Telephone Company, which ultimately chose not to develop the technology.

Designing the Solution

In early 1885, Woods saw an article in *Scientific American* describing an induction communication system invented by a man named Lucius Phelps. The system had already been used on a section of railroad to allow telegraph communication with moving trains.

The article was a shock to Woods, who was concerned that he would lose the chance to profit from his invention. He scrambled to file for a patent on induction telegraphy.

Phelps had filed for the same patent, so the US Patent Office conducted an investigation. Although Woods had filed later than Phelps, he was able to prove that he had originated the idea of using induction to communicate with moving trains in early 1881, well before Phelps.

In 1887, the Patent Office awarded the patent to Woods. Even before Woods won the patent battle, the case had attracted media attention, as well as the attention of some prominent Cincinnati businessmen who became interested in backing the talented inventor. Woods joined forces with them, founding the Woods Electrical Company in 1886.

Woods quickly became dissatisfied with his backers. He wanted to develop Woods Electrical into a business, but his backers, who had control of the business decisions, wanted only to sell his patents to other companies. Woods, who was supposed to receive a salary from Woods Electrical, was paid irregularly.

By 1890, Woods had extricated himself from his agreement with Woods Electrical and moved to New York City. Although the induction patents were controlled by Woods Electrical, Woods hoped to find different backers for some of his new ideas.

Investors were scarce, and Woods again descended into poverty. In August 1891, Woods saw an advertisement for the American Patent Agency, which promised to help inventors sell their work. Intrigued, Woods visited American Patent, where he met James Zerbe, the manager. Zerbe impressed Woods, who entered into a partnership with him later that month. Woods quickly regretted this decision when he discovered that Zerbe was filing, under Woods's name, patents that contained the ideas of other inventors. By October, Woods and Zerbe were getting into fistfights at the office. Woods broke off the partnership and testified before the Patent Office against the filings that Zerbe had made under his name.

Zerbe attempted to market an electric railway system that Woods had invented, building a demonstration rail at Coney Island in Brooklyn. The railway, unveiled in February 1892, drew considerable attention because it was one of the first to rely on a third rail. The

A New Kind of Communication

In the 1880s, Woods invented a system to communicate with moving elevator or train cars. It used a natural phenomenon called electromagnetic induction. Such induction was first observed in 1831, when Michael Faraday (1791–1867) moved a magnet through a coil of wire and discovered that the magnet created an electrical current in the wire.

Woods realized that a magnetic field could be created inside a moving car using an electrical system. The car could then be surrounded by wires, strung up on either side of a railroad track, and the magnetic field would create an electrical current in those wires. Since the electrical system within the car could be turned on and off, the magnetic field could be turned on and off. As a result, the electrical current in the wires outside the moving car could be turned on and off from inside the car. As long as the car was moving, electrical impulses from inside the car could be transferred to wires outside it; the two systems never had to touch.

Radio had not been invented at this point. Without wireless communication, designing a reliable system that would allow people outside a moving car to speak to those inside it was almost impossible. Woods realized that the very motion of the car made communication through induction possible.

third rail, which forms a part of most modern subway systems, is a grounding rail that carries the electricity needed to power a train. Previous trolley systems had relied on overhead wires to carry electricity, but these wires were constantly exposed to wind and weather and, as a result, broke often.

Woods took out advertisements in newspapers informing the public that Zerbe had built the railroad using ideas he did not own. Zerbe retaliated by charging Woods with libel. The libel case went to trial in April 1892, and events began to favor Woods: he was quickly acquitted, with the jury granting him full control over his electric railway inventions.

Woods was not the only inventor Zerbe had treated badly. Following Woods's successful defense, he and a group of other inventors began a campaign to have Zerbe barred from representing inventors at the Patent Office. (At the time, anyone could act as a patent solicitor who had not been specifically forbidden to do so by the office.) In November 1893, they succeeded, and Zerbe was banned from patent practice.

Applying the Solution

Ironically, Woods's problems with Zerbe probably benefited him in the long run. Despite its illicit origins, the Coney Island electrical railway built by Zerbe attracted considerable media coverage. Also, Woods's efforts to ban Zerbe from patent practice, in addition to his willingness to testify against his own patents to protect other inventors, helped to connect him to the inventing community. The libel trial put a spotlight on Woods's talents as an inventor. By 1896, the *New York Times* was referring to Woods as "one of the best known colored men" in the city.

By that point, Woods was able to attract the interest of legitimate technology companies that would actually develop his inventions and compensate him for his patents. Woods eventually developed very close relationships with General Electric Company and Westinghouse Electric and Manufacturing Company; he had more than forty patents to his name by the time of his death in January 1910 at the age of fifty-four.

The Impact of the Solution on Society

Woods continued to focus on railroad technology later in his life, particularly the electric trains that eventually became subway systems, an interest that dovetailed with General Electric's and Westinghouse's business strategies. In addition to the third rail, Woods helped to develop the automated air brake, which greatly improved train safety; and he made numerous other technological improvements to electric trains, including developing methods to better regulate their speed.

Today Woods's memory lives on in modern subway systems, which greatly benefited from his designs. His attention to detail and careful planning helped make train travel safer, too. Woods was an inspiration to the early train industry. He proved that in order to succeed you should conquer obstacles and fight for the right course of action.

Timeline

1856
Granville Woods born; grows up in Columbus, Ohio

1881
Woods works on using induction as a communications tool

1883
Woods patents a steam boiler

1886
Woods founds the Woods Electrical Company

1890
Woods moves to New York City

1892
A railway system based on Woods's ideas is demonstrated at Coney Island

1910
Woods dies

Inventors of the Modern Airplane

Orville Wright and Wilbur Wright

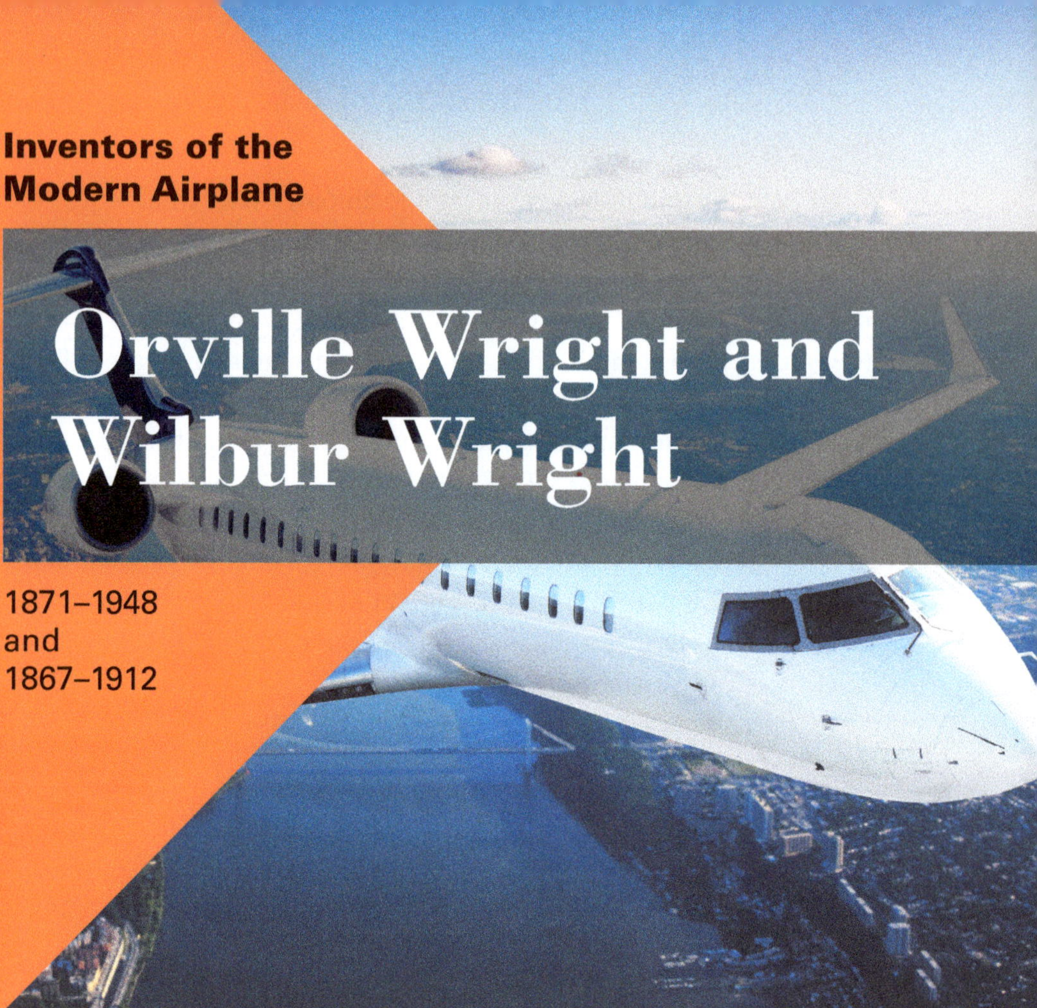

1871–1948
and
1867–1912

Since early human history, people have been fascinated with the power of flight. Many ancient myths relate to humans wishing to fly. However, it wasn't until the twentieth century that significant strides were taken to making that dream a reality. Prior to the early 1900s, aircraft had been invented—there was the kite, hot air balloons, and gliders (unpowered airplanes)—yet a manned, powered device had not been made. Two brothers from Dayton, Ohio, would change that and would be forever remembered in history as the creators of the first modern airplane. Sketches of imagined flying machines cover journals and scrolls of historic figures. Most well known were the drawings done by Leonardo da Vinci (1452–1519) in the fifteenth and sixteenth centuries.

Inventing Together

Wilbur and Orville Wright were two of five children born to Milton Wright, a bishop of the Church of the United Brethren in Christ, and his wife, Susan. Wilbur, the couple's third child, was born in 1867, on a farm outside Millville, Indiana. Orville was born four years later, after the family had moved to Dayton. Independent and businesslike from an early age, the two Wright brothers earned pocket money by selling homemade toys. A toy their father bought for them in 1878, a model helicopter powered by a rubber band, sowed a seed in their minds for an invention that would change history.

In 1886, at the age of fifteen, Orville Wright started his own school newspaper, *The Midget*, after his family gave him a printing press as a gift. Soon, the brothers had opened a print shop and built large presses of superb quality for other local printers. By 1889, Orville was publishing Dayton's weekly newspaper, *West Side News*, with his brother as editor, and charging 40 cents for a year's subscription. Their efforts to publish *The Evening Item,* a daily paper, were short-lived, largely because Dayton already had twelve other newspapers. Their next venture was more successful: their superb mechanical skills led them to open a bicycle shop in December 1892. The Wright Cycle Company had its own workshop and by 1896 was manufacturing bicycles for sale or rent. The brothers were known not only for their skills but also for their appearance, wearing suits and bow ties even when fixing tires or straightening spokes.

Defining the Problem

On August 10, 1896, the brothers and the world were shocked by the death of German engineer Otto Lilienthal (1848–1896), who died after crashing one of his experimental gliders. Often described as a "birdman," Lilienthal helped to prove that humans could fly by strapping enormous wooden wings to his body and jumping from a hill. The Wrights had taken a close interest in flight ever since their father bought them a model of an early helicopter almost twenty years before. Soon after hearing of Lilienthal's death, they turned their attention to making a flying machine of their own.

The brothers started off by poring over books in the library, reading about all those who had tried to fly before them. They read about pioneers like the Montgolfiers, two French brothers who flew the world's first hot air balloon in 1783. Hot air balloons are difficult to steer, however. Gliders, which became popular during the second half of the nineteenth century, interested the Wrights more because they were easier to control.

The Wright Brothers: Wilbur (*left*) and Orville (*right*), ca. 1910

During 1899, the Wrights read all the material they could find on flight and started writing to people who they thought might help, including Samuel P. Langley (1834–1906), head of the Smithsonian Institution, who had already flown large model airplanes. That summer, they built a 2-foot (0.6 m) kite with wings to try out their ideas. Dayton was flat and mostly windless, so by November they were writing to the US Weather Bureau asking where the best windy places were to test gliders. Their most important series of letters was begun on May 13, 1900, when Wilbur wrote to Octave Chanute (1832–1910), a world-famous engineer who helped early aviators. Chanute offered to meet the Wright brothers and exchanged several hundred letters with them over the next ten years.

Designing the Solution

Encouraged by Chanute's enthusiasm, the Wrights made their first serious experiments from the windy Kill Devil Hill, near the village of Kitty Hawk in North Carolina. Their first glider was a 10-foot (3 m) biplane with two wings, one stacked above the other, but they flew it mostly as a kite, without a pilot, to see how it behaved. A glider has no engine, so it needs big wings to generate enough lift (upward force) to support its own weight plus the weight of the pilot. The Wrights' first glider had wings that were too small, so it flew no more than 300 feet (91 m) before crashing to the ground. The following year, in 1901, they made a glider with wings almost twice the size of the original, but to the Wrights' great disappointment, it flew only about 100 feet (30 m) farther.

"The person who merely watches the flight of a bird gathers the impression that the bird has nothing to think of but the flapping of its wings. As a matter of fact, this is a very small part of its mental labor ... We only learn to appreciate it when we try to imitate it."
—Wilbur Wright

That fall, they discovered the problem. The brothers were designing their gliders using numeric data that Langley and Lilienthal had worked out—and the data seemed to be wrong. Having decided that they needed better data, they built a **wind tunnel** out of a wooden box, a gasoline engine, and an old fan. With a measuring device made from an old hacksaw blade and some bicycle spokes, they tested more than two hundred different wing shapes inside the wind tunnel until they hit upon the best design. With a new glider in 1902, they found they could now fly more than 600 feet (183 m) and stay airborne for almost thirty seconds. Although much trial and error was involved, the Wrights were extremely scientific in their approach. They made almost one thousand flights, taking photographs of their tests and recording all the details in notebooks.

The Wrights' glider still relied on wind power. During late 1902 and 1903, the brothers started to wonder how they could make a powered airplane that did not need any wind. The obvious answer was to use a gasoline engine like the ones that had recently been invented for automobiles. Gas engines were huge and heavy; how could an airplane carry one and still get off the ground? When the Wrights asked engineering companies to help them build a lightweight engine, no one knew how. In the true spirit of invention, the brothers returned to their bicycle workshop in Dayton and built their own engine. By September 1903, their new plane, *Flyer* or *Kitty Hawk Flyer*, was ready (the brothers themselves often called it "the Whopper flying machine"). They returned to Kitty Hawk and spent several weeks preparing to fly. Finally, on December 17 at 10:35 a.m., Orville Wright took to the air. In the twelve brief seconds that he stayed aloft, he made history as the first person ever to fly an engine-powered airplane.

Applying the Solution

The Wright brothers' first powered flight was an important scientific experiment as well as a historic achievement. It proved that a powered airplane could carry a person through the sky. However, *Flyer* traveled less than 300 yards (274 m), a distance that was not much of an improvement over their gliders. The Wright brothers knew they would

The First to Fly

On May 6, 1896, seven years before the Wright brothers made their historic flight, Samuel Pierpont Langley flew a 16-foot (5 m) model airplane for about ninety seconds across the Potomac River. Langley's extraordinary plane was powered by a steam engine and launched from a riverboat by a catapult, but it could not carry a pilot. The years that followed the Wrights' success saw some debate about whether Langley had really invented the "flying machine" first. That question became a source of great annoyance to the Wrights.

Langley, who was the secretary of the Smithsonian Institution and one of the most distinguished scientists in the United States, could not have been more different from the Wright brothers, the two unknown bicycle makers from Dayton, Ohio. He enjoyed government backing for his plane, but the Wrights had to struggle to finance their own experiments from the profits of their bicycle shop.

However, whereas the Wrights had achieved glory, Langley's efforts had ended in bitter disappointment. Despite having $50,000 have to fly much farther, and they set about making an improved version of *Flyer*. By the following summer, they were flying almost 3 miles (5 km) for up to five minutes at a time. Hardly anyone knew what they were doing; the Wrights decided to keep their work secret until they had protected their invention. Meanwhile, they improved the plane's design and made more trials.

In 1905, they twice offered their invention to the US government—and twice they were turned down. By this time, the plane could fly 24.5 miles (39.4 km) in thirty-nine minutes at an average speed of 38 miles per hour (61 kmh). In May 1906, a patent was granted to the Wright brothers for their "Flying Machine." More confident now about showing their invention, they began making demonstration flights in the United States and Europe.

The year 1908 brought great success when the US War Department finally accepted the Wrights' offer to build planes, but disaster struck, too. During a test flight on September 17, Orville Wright's airplane crashed to the ground from a height of 75 feet (23 m),

from the War Department to develop person-carrying airplanes, and a similar sum from the Smithsonian, Langley's failures became something of a joke. One government official told the newspapers: "You tell Langley for me that the only thing he ever made fly was government money."

After Langley's death in 1906, the leaders of the Smithsonian remained fiercely loyal to him: they insisted he had built a machine "capable" of flying years before the Wright brothers and deserved credit.

Orville Wright considered this an insult and demanded an apology. None was forthcoming, so instead of lending *Flyer* to the Smithsonian, as many people would have expected, he had it shipped to the Science Museum in London, England. It stayed there until 1942, when the Smithsonian Institution issued an apology. The plane was promptly shipped back to the United States and to the Smithsonian, where it is a permanent part of the collection at the National Air and Space Museum.

severely injuring him and killing his passenger, Lieutenant Thomas Selfridge—the first person to die in an airplane accident.

The following year, 1909, the Wrights set up an airplane manufacturing company in New York City, with Wilbur as president and Orville as vice president. They also allowed some industrialists in Germany to set up a company, Wright GmbH, to make their planes under license in return for a large payment. Almost from the start, much of their energy was taken up fighting rivals who seemed to be copying their ideas. Their first target was Glenn Curtiss (1878–1930),

Tackling Wing Warping

In Wilbur Wright's remarkable letter to engineer Octave Chanute, he declared, "For some years I have been afflicted with the belief that flight is possible to man. My disease has increased in severity and I feel that it will soon cost me an increased amount of money if not my life." After years of study and experimentation, the Wright brothers' "disease" bore fruit when *Flyer* took to the air on December 17, 1903. Thinking of their plane as a glider, the Wrights had chosen the windiest place they could find, Kitty Hawk in North Carolina, with steep dunes to help them take off and soft sand to cushion their landing. In fact, their biggest achievement was to prove that airplanes could fly without any wind at all.

Gliders stay in the air because they have airfoil wings: seen from the side, the top of an airfoil is curved and the bottom is flat. Air has to move farther over the top of the wing than under the bottom, so the air that travels over the top of the wing has to go faster to keep up. This fast-moving air creates an upward force (lift) that keeps a glider airborne. A glider relies on wind to blow over the wings and create lift. The Wright brothers realized they could achieve the same effect by putting an engine and two propellers at the back of their plane so that, in effect, it made its own wind. The propellers created a backdraft of air that pushed the airplane forward. Its wings created lift and pushed it up into the air.

soon to become a famous pilot, who started to manufacture his own airplane in June 1909. Other patent suits followed in both the United States and Europe, though they did not really solve the problem. The legal wrangling over their invention finally ended in 1917 when their patent expired; the US government refused to renew it because competition would lead to better airplanes.

The Impact of the Solution on Society

Legal battles and other business worries took their toll on Wilbur Wright. Suffering from typhoid fever, he died on May 30, 1912, at the age of forty-five.

Becoming airborne was one thing, but staying aloft was quite another. In his letter to Octave Chanute of May 1900, Wilbur Wright explained how he had watched buzzards steering themselves and controlling their flight by twisting the tips of their wings. This was the inspiration for *Flyer's* steering system, which the Wrights called "wing warping," and which used cables running from the pilot's waist to the wings. To steer the plane, the pilot wriggled one way or the other so the cables pulled the back edge of one wing up and the other wing down. This made more lift on one side of the plane than on the other and steered the plane to the left or to the right. It seemed a strange and frightening system, but it worked.

An airplane cannot reach speed and become airborne immediately, so the Wright brothers still needed a means to launch *Flyer* into the air. They achieved launch by mounting the plane on a truck that ran along a short length of wooden railroad, which they had previously laid down on the sand dunes at Kill Devil Hill. With the engine buzzing and the propeller turning, they let the plane roll down the track until it was going just fast enough to lift itself in the air. Wilbur, running alongside, steadied one wingtip with his hands. Strapped in the pilot's position and facing forward, Orville flew into the future—and straight into history.

This image shows the first flight of *Flyer* in 1903.

For the next three years, Orville ran the Wright Company alone, but in 1915 he sold his stake and retired from the airplane-making business. From then on, he led a quieter life, tinkering with machines and inventions, collecting awards, promoting aviation, and spending time with his friends and family in Dayton and at a country retreat in Georgian Bay near Lake Huron in Ontario, Canada. Orville died of a heart attack in Dayton on January 30, 1948.

During the twentieth century, airplanes revolutionized around-the-world transportation as much as railroads had changed travel over land a century earlier. Pilots were soon flying farther, faster, and for longer—crossing oceans, setting records, and effectively making the world smaller. World War I (1914–1918) greatly speeded the development of better airplanes, as rival nations raced to gain advantage in the air.

World War II (1939–1945) produced a dramatic leap forward when British engineer Frank Whittle (1907–1996) and his German rival Hans Pabst von Ohain (1911–1998) produced the jet engine that was soon flying airplanes at the speed of sound (around 660 mph, or 1,062 kmh). The jet engine arrived too late to make much impact on the war itself, but it certainly changed travel in the decades that followed. From the 1950s onward, jet airplanes led to a new era of inexpensive, international air travel. At the same time, rocket engineers were sending the first satellites and people into space. All these developments built on the Wright brothers' accomplishments.

Today air travel is still an essential part of navigating the world. Every year, millions of men, women, and children take flights to all corners of the globe. The Wright brothers' accomplishments have truly changed society in ways they themselves could not have imagined. While Wilbur and Orville Wright built their invention on the backs of other creations that came before them, they successfully proved that air travel was possible. Likewise, their desire to enable people to achieve flight was recognized and celebrated, and their names will forever be remembered in aviation and world history.

Timeline

1867
Wilbur Wright born near Millville, Indiana

1871
Orville Wright born in Dayton, Ohio

1892
The Wright Cycle Company is founded

1896
The Wright brothers begin studying flight

1900
The Wright brothers build and crash their first glider

1903
The Wright brothers build *Flyer* and successfully test it

1906
The Wright brothers patent their flying machine

1909
The Wright Brothers found an airplane manufacturing company

1912
Wilbur Wright dies

1915
Orville Wright retires

1948
Orville Wright dies

Glossary

altitude The height above ground.

assembly line A process popularized by Henry Ford that presented parts for a project on a conveyor belt. One person put each part together before it advanced to the next stage of the assembling process.

counter-rotate Turning in opposite ways.

czar The name for a Russian king.

dirigible Airship.

draftsman Someone who draws technical plans of a project.

draisine A two-wheeled vehicle, usually made of wood and operated by walking or running, that inspired the modern-day bicycle.

ferry To transport goods from one place to another.

fossil fuel Any material, such as oil, gas, or coal, that is formed in the earth, usually from dead or decaying animals. It can be used as a source of energy.

gear A wheel with teeth that meshes together with other wheels of its kind.

glazier Another name for a glassmaker.

hydrocarbon A complex chemical formed from the elements hydrogen and carbon.

induction A process by which electricity is created.

jet engine An aircraft engine powered by a mixture of hot fuel and gas roaring through it.

Mercator projection A way of representing the three-dimensional earth on a two-dimensional sheet of paper using lines of latitude and longitude.

mode A method; technique.

niche A space in a marketplace mostly unexplored by entrepreneurs or businesspeople.

nonconformist A person who does not follow rules of a church.

piston A rod that fits snugly inside a cylinder but can slide freely up and down.

protégé A person taken on as an apprentice and eventual inheritor of a business or trade.

prototype The first example of a product; a model of an invention.

steam engine A device, similar to a gigantic kettle, that is fueled by coal and uses the energy in steam to drive powerful machines.

temporary memory The impermanent memory that computers use to function when they are on.

thermodynamics The science of how heat moves.

versatile Adaptable; excelling in many things.

wind tunnel An enclosed chamber with a fan at one end.

Further Information

Introduction to Transportation Technology

Books

Cox, Kevin J. *100 Great Moments of Science: From Archimedes to Einstein and Beyond*. Seattle, WA: Island Light Books, 2011.

Houston, Rob, and Chopra Virien, eds. *DK Eyewitness: Transportation*. New York: DK Publishing, 2012.

Websites

America on the Move: Transportation History
amhistory.si.edu/onthemove/themes/story_48_1.html

Horrible Histories: Pioneers of Transportation
www.youtube.com/watch?v=NLL2Txs8kCg

Mary Anderson: Inventor of the Windshield Wiper

Books

Latta, Sara L. *The Woman Who Invented Windshield Wipers: Mary Anderson and Her Wonderful Invention*. Inventors at Work! New York: Enslow, 2014.

Thimmesh, Catherine. *Girls Think of Everything: Stories of Ingenious Inventions by Women*. New York: Houghton Mifflin, 2000.

Websites

Illuminating Moments in American History: Windshield Wipers
www.youtube.com/watch?v=7mugNKIcano

On This Day: Mary Anderson Patents Windshield Wiper
www.history.com/this-day-in-history/mary-anderson-patents-windshield-wiper

Karl Benz: Inventor of the Gasoline Automobile

Books

Hennessey, Kathryn, ed. *Car: The Definitive Visual History of the Automobile*. New York: DK Publishing, 2011.

Legate, Trevor. *The Ultimate History of Mercedes-Benz*. New York: Parragon, 2005.

Watson, Peter. *The German Genius: Europe's Third Renaissance, the Second Scientific Revolution, and the Twentieth Century*. New York: Harper Perennial, 2011.

Websites **History of Automaker Mercedes Benz**
www.youtube.com/watch?v=V2jmfbtSJUo

The Official Website of Mercedes-Benz
www.mbusa.com/mercedes/index

Allen Breed: Inventor of the Air Bag

Book Rose, Sharon, and Neil Schlager. *How Things Are Made: From Automobiles to Zippers*. New York: Black Dog & Leventhal Publishers, 2003.

Websites **Explain That Stuff: How Do Air Bags Work?**
www.explainthatstuff.com/airbags.html

I Didn't Know That: Air Bags
www.youtube.com/watch?v=SSz6y-W-R_A

Gottlieb Daimler:
Pioneer Automobile Manufacturer, Inventor of the Motorcycle

Books Parissien, Steven. *The Life of the Automobile: The Complete History of the Motor Car*. New York: Thomas Dunne Books, 2013.

Dunne, Jemima, ed. *Motorcycle: The Definitive Visual History*. New York: DK Publishing, 2012.

Websites **Biography of Gottlieb Daimler**
www.britannica.com/EBchecked/topic/149896/Gottlieb-Daimler

The Official Website of Daimler
www.daimler.com

Rudolf Diesel: Inventor of the Diesel Engine

Books McDonnell, Greg. *Locomotives: The Modern Diesel and Electric Reference*. Erin, Ontario, Canada: Boston Mills Press, 2008.

Smil, Vaclav. *Prime Movers of Globalization: The History and Impact of Diesel Engines and Gas Turbines*. Cambridge, MA: MIT, 2010.

Websites **Biography of Rudolf Diesel**
www.britannica.com/EBchecked/topic/162711/Rudolf-Diesel

Further Information

How Stuff Works: How Rudolf Diesel Changed the World
www.youtube.com/watch?v=rB9LKj2dfaY

Henry Ford: Inventor of the Model T and Moving Assembly Line

Books

El Nabli, Dina. *Time for Kids: Henry Ford.* Time for Kids Biographies. New York: HarperCollins, 2008.

Snow, Richard. *I Invented the Modern Age: The Rise of Henry Ford.* New York: Simon & Schuster, 2013.

Websites

Henry Ford Changes the World: The History of the Model T Ford
www.youtube.com/watch?v=RDjRxKJJ__I

The Official Website of Ford Car Dealership
www.ford.com

Ivan A. Getting: Inventor of the Global Positioning System

Books

Bray, Hiawatha. *You Are Here: From the Compass to GPS, the History and Future of How We Find Ourselves.* New York: Basic Books, 2014.

Easton, Richard D., and Eric F. Frazer. *GPS Declassified.* Lincoln, NE: Potomac Books, 2013.

Websites

A Brief History of GPS
www.techhive.com/article/2000276/a-brief-history-of-gps.html

How GPS Works
www.youtube.com/watch?v=loRQiNFzT0k

Pierre Michaux: Developer of the Bicycle

Books

Ambrose, Tom. *The History of Cycling in Fifty Bikes: From the Velocipede to the Pinarello: The Bicycles That Have Shaped the World.* Emmaus, PA: Rodale Books, 2013.

Newson, Alex. *Fifty Bicycles That Changed the World.* London: Conran, 2013.

Websites

America on the Move: The Development of the Bicycle
amhistory.si.edu/onthemove/themes/story_69_2.html

Thoroughly Modern: The Bicycle
www.youtube.com/watch?v=lBitle48_LM&list=PL_jqgKoUzzRB5tpMJ1kQVr7-Wv51tKP0B

Joseph-Michel Montgolfier and Jacques-Étienne Montgolfier: Inventors of the Hot Air Balloon

Books

Becker, Jean. *Hot Air Balloons: History, Evolution, and Great Adventures*. New York: White Star Publishers, 2011.

Holmes, Richard. *Falling Upwards: How We Took to the Air: An Unconventional History of Ballooning*. New York: Vintage Books, 2014.

Websites

Ballooning History
www.nationalballoonmuseum.com/Exhibits/BallooningHistory.aspx

Learning to Fly a Hot Air Balloon
www.businessinsider.com/flying-a-hot-air-balloon-2014-10

Thomas Newcomen: Inventor of the Steam Engine

Books

Crump, Thomas. *A Brief History of the Age of Steam: From the First Engine to the Boats and Railways*. Philadelphia: Running Press, 2007.

Rosen, William. *The Most Powerful Idea in the World: A Story of Steam, Industry, and Invention*. Chicago: University of Chicago Press, 2012.

Websites

Biography of Thomas Newcomen
www.bbc.co.uk/history/historic_figures/newcomen_thomas.shtml

Steam Engine Drives a Revolution
www.history.com/topics/industrial-revolution/videos/steam-engine-drives-transportation-revolution

Further Information

Brennan Olson and Scott Olson: Inventors of Rollerblades

Book Rompella, Natalie. *Famous Firsts: The Trendsetters, Groundbreakers, and Risk-Takers Who Got America Moving!* Montreal, Quebec: Lobster Press, 2007.

Websites **The Daily Spin: Rollerblade History**
www.youtube.com/watch?v=_QVDtvcqMgI

The Official Website of Rollerblade
www.rollerblade.com/usa

Igor Sikorsky: Inventor of the Modern Helicopter

Books Sikorsky, Sergei I. *The Sikorsky Legacy.* Images of Aviation. Charleston, SC: Arcadia Publishing, 2007.

Stadiem, William. *Jet Set: The People, the Planes, the Glamour, and the Romance in Aviation's Glory Years.* New York: Ballantine, 2014.

Websites **Almanac: Igor Sikorsky**
www.youtube.com/watch?v=DVJV2AaRoWQ

World's First Helicopter Ride
connecticuthistory.org/worlds-first-helicopter-today-in-history

George Stephenson: Pioneer of Railroads

Books Davies, Hunter. *George Stephenson: The Remarkable Life of the Founder of the Railway.* Stroud, Gloucestershire, England: The History Press, 2013.

Wolmar, Christian. *The Iron Road: An Illustrated History of the Railroad.* New York: DK Publishing, 2014.

Websites **Historic Figures: George Stephenson**
www.bbc.co.uk/history/historic_figures/stephenson_george.shtml

Stephenson's Rocket Animation
www.bbc.co.uk/history/british/victorians/launch_ani_rocket.shtml

Robert Watson-Watt: Pioneer of Radar

Books Holland, James. *The Battle of Britain: Five Months That Changed History; May–October 1940.* New York: St. Martin's Press, 2010.

Watson, Raymond C., Jr. *Radar Origins Worldwide: History of Its Evolution in 13 Nations Through World War II.* Bloomington, IN: Trafford Publishing, 2009.

Websites **BBC: Robert Watson-Watts, Pioneer of Radar**
www.bbc.com/news/uk-scotland-tayside-central-27393558

Explain That Stuff: How Radar Works
www.explainthatstuff.com/radar.html

Granville Woods: Inventor of Devices for Electric Railways

Books Walker, Jonathan. *Granville Taylor Woods: The First Black American Who Was Granted Forty-Nine Patents.* Bloomington, IN: Xlibris Corp, 2011.

Walker, Robin. *Blacks and Science Volume Three: African American Contributions to Science and Technology.* Seattle, WA: Reklaw Education, 2013.

Websites **Biography of Granville T. Woods**
www.biography.com/people/granville-t-woods-9536481

Spotlight on Granville Woods
www.youtube.com/watch?v=K2bIdD7SDQs

Orville Wright and Wilbur Wright: Inventors of the Modern Airplane

Books *Aircraft: The Definitive Visual History.* New York: DK Publishing, 2013.

Goldstone, Lawrence. *The Wright Brothers, Glenn Curtiss, and the Battle to Control the Skies.* New York: Ballantine, 2014.

Grant, R. G. *Flight: The Complete History.* New York: DK Publishing, 2007.

Websites **Airplanes That Transformed Aviation**
www.airspacemag.com/history-of-flight/airplanes-that-transformed-aviation-46502830/?no-ist

The Wright Brothers' First Flight
www.youtube.com/watch?v=T5o-fhBKf8Y

Index

Page numbers in **boldface** are illustrations. Entries in **boldface** are glossary terms.

Index